The Evil Queen

THE
EVIL
QUEEN

A PORNOLEXICOLOGY

Benjamin L. Perez

Spuyten Duyvil
1-800-886-5304
http://spuytenduyvil.net

Threefold Dedication:

for Donald Barthelme
(who wrote *Snow White*)

for Webster's Ninth New Collegiate Dictionary

and for You

Every other author may aspire to praise; the lexicographer can only hope to escape reproach.
                                        —Doctor Johnson

PROLOGUE

First, dear reader, allow me to impart this advice: READ THIS WORK ALOUD. Read it aloud and read it slowly. Like nectar on the tongue, or a cock in the mouth, savor each sentence, savor before swallowing. Preferably, read it to another. Indeed, run out, abduct a nun, strip her naked, bind her to a four-poster bed, lie beside her, and read this work aloud (it is best to abduct a nun—believe me, priests are rarely as rewarding). True, gagging the Sister is a must, but do not blindfold her. It is best that she read along as it is read aloud. That is what I did, and I grew i m m e n s e l y from the experience.

Novel, memoirs, textbook, manifesto? What exactly, dear reader, do you hold in your dirty hands? Asmodeus calls it "Sublime Smut;" Beelzebub prefers "Profound Pornography"—"Transgressive Literature" is the term of choice among most devils (everyone in Hell is a literary critic). I thought of proposing the term "Linguistic Deconstruction of Evil," but I always seem to forget the difference between DECONSTRUCTION and RECONSTRUCTION (the terms make more sense when applied to engineering).

Read the work aloud, and read it slowly — and do not forget the nun!

MEPHISTOPHELES

CONTENTS

PART ONE

Crucifixion

[sound of church bells behind black curtain — curtain rises]

CLITORIDES

SHE is very tall. She is very thin. A clitoris protrudes from ten separate parts of her body. From the front, moving top to bottom (to mock the crucifix): Eve's apple, left nipple, right nipple, navel, and top of cunt. From the back, again, moving top to bottom (crucifix inverted): nape, small of back, left cheek (center), right cheek (center), and, of course, the anus. Each clitoris being one inch, making ten inches in all.

(pink pink thorns on a white white stem)

She demands the greatest attention for each.

GRAPH

Eve's Apple	•			•		Nape
Nipples	•	•		•		Small of Back
Navel	•		•	•		Buttocks
Cunt	•			•		Anus

Her hair is Bible-Black. Her skin is skeleton-white.

CRUCIFER

AZRAEL

YOU never grow tired of The Evil Queen.

You die when she is away.

You are born when she is near.

You have never understood the expression:

I would die for you.

If you died for The Evil Queen, then you would be away from her:

Forever.

The ancient Hebrews (and you must recall they had no Heaven) are reported to have felt that Death was worse than Life for this and this reason chiefly:

That they would be even further from their God.

Indeed, a brilliant people.

SHEOL

EUPHEMISM

SHE is a banshee running through the castle.

(*s c r e e e e e e e e e e e c h ! ! !*)

"Words!" She tears the curtains from the window.

"Words!" She kicks the door off its hinges.

"Words! Words! Words!" She pulls and pulls at her black black hair.

"Vulgar! Vernacular! Obscene!" She crashes a vase against the wall.

"Cunt!   Fuck!   Slut!   Whore!"

"These, do you hear me, these words have Life!"

"Pussy? No power."

"Make Love? No bite."

"Coquette? Too much lace."

"Hooker? Oh yes, hooker! At last we are getting close!"

"The further one stands from Life, the less one offends while speaking. Hence, the power of blasphemy!"

"Civilization promotes fair speech!"

"Civilization engenders Death!"

"Pyramids lie! Cathedrals lie! Skyscrapers lie!"

"Lies ! ! !"

"Lies ! ! !"

"Lies ! ! !"

She takes a deep breath:

> *And the name of God can never be spoken,*
> *no doubt the source of all obscenity!*

EXECRATION

D I L U V I U M

SHE has sent you to do some washing. Sometimes you wash her dishes. Sometimes you wash her hair. Sometimes you wash her clothes. And sometimes, sometimes, when you are very lucky, when you have been very good, she allows you to wash her anus after she returns from the privy. But not today. Today you wash the castle walls.

There are few activities as satisfying as washing. Take these castle walls. So dusty, so dirty, so in need of washing. Few people possess not only the skill, but the will, to conduct the perfect wash. There is something magical, indeed, something redemptive, about the act. Take all the impurities, all the imperfections, and wash them away.

Away! Away! Away!

The water on your hands. The suds. The bubbles. Like Venus emerging from the sea: Clean   Fresh   New.   (this is your role)

You thrust the bucket into the air, high high into the air, so the water, the water, rains down upon you, water runs down the castle walls.

She has chosen you because no one can wash better. And you have chosen her because no one has more to wash.

There, all the walls are clean, no longer dull, but shining. Almost like mirrors. Yes, a castle surrounded by shining mirrors. You especially like the tiny rainbows, how they are dancing, to and fro, to and fro.

And only 18 hours work.

E X T R E M E   U N C T I O N

DAILY MISSAL

THE chapters of a novel that The Evil Queen wrote in Latin:

Chapter I   Aqua Et Igni Interdictus
             [Forbidden To Be Furnished With Water and Fire]

Chapter II   Odi Et Amo
             [I Hate And I Love]

Chapter III Aegri Somnia
             [A Sick Man's Dreams]

Chapter IV   Vade Retro Me, Satana
             [Get Thee Behind Me, Satan]

Chapter V   Credo Quia Absurdum Est
             [I Believe It Because It Is Absurd]

Chapter VI   Pallida Mors
             [Pale Death]

EXEGESIS

L U B A

The Certainty and Conformity of The Evil Queen: "I know who I am to love and hate," The Evil Queen says, without a hint of hesitation.

Hence, she knows who is to love you.
Hence, she knows who is to hate you.

Always confident. Always sure.

Still, she is not without a sense of humor.

(she just winked)

H A Z

APOTHEGM

THE EVIL QUEEN is renowned for her sayings. In fact, even her enemies know her maxims by heart. Here is but a sampling from her best known:

Those who fear the water have never swam.

The one who is in love is seldom at ease.

The more beautiful the bird, the more the trapper longs to cage it.

A woman's sword is her looks.

Priests and wives give the worst advice.

A lover can never be loved from a distance.

Fresh meat wets the lips.

Better to be in Heaven with The Devil then with Jesus in Hell.

The wetter one's finger, the more sugar one may lift.

Those who love the water are blessed if they drown.

LOGION

K H A R Y B D I S

THERE is a river of white that is the skin of The Evil Queen. A creature dwells in the river. Ten horns peek up through the waves.

Sometimes you brave the currents. Sometimes you swim with the beast.

At first, the currents were too strong. Beast or no beast, the waves were too much.

But you persisted.

Just your hands at first. Your fingers wet against the rush of the stream. Then your legs, one at a time, still holding onto land.

Finally, you took the plunge.

(your first swim nearly killed you)

The mighty flux of the river. The rush of the mighty white. The horns cutting your hands. And you, struggling to get away. Your red hands slapping the white. The monster pulling you, pulling you down, down-down-down, pulling you under the alabaster swirl.

So you held your breath, and kicked and kicked and kicked.

Later, you found yourself on land, coughing, coughing, spitting up the white.

(you did not wait five minutes to re-enter that river)

C O R N U A

ROSERY

THIS is on the mind of The Evil Queen:

Bring my wine!
Bring my roses!

Bring my red! red! wine!
Bring my red! red! roses!

Atop her dining table:

                    L   A   R   G   E
                      clear grail
                      filled with
                        red red
                         wine,
                          six
                       red roses
                    emerging from it.

Atop her writing desk:

L   A   R   G   E
clear grail
filled with
red red
wine,
six
red roses
emerging from it.

Red wine aging in her red barrels in the cellar.
Red roses burgeoning in her red rose garden.

!!! RED !!!

!!! RED !!!

!!! RED !!!

!!! RED !!!

!!! RED !!!

You are running to her bed chamber!

Running, running fast!

You are bringing her sangria!

Running, running fast!

You are biting nine red roses!

Running, running, running fast ! ! !

S A N G R I A

PULCHRITUDE

THE DIVINITY OF THE EVIL QUEEN

PRINCIPAL MODE OF DEIFICATION:

HER MIRROR

APOTHEOSIS

FRANCOPHILE

IN addition to the privilege of washing the anus of The Evil Queen, you benefit from French lessons:

FRONT

•

Eve's Apple
la belle dame sans merci
(the beautiful lady without mercy)

•

(Right) Nipple
cherchez la femme
(look for the woman)

•

(Left) Nipple
beaux yeux
(beautiful eyes)
[beautiful face]

•

Navel
peine forte et due
(strong and hard punishment)
[torture]

•

Cunt
j'y suis, j'y reste
(here I am, here I stay)

And if you please The Evil Queen (and you want to please her), you are allowed to proceed to lesson two:

BACK

•

Nape
bon appetit
(good appetite)
[enjoy your meal]

•

Small of Back
volupte
(pleasure)
[sensuality]

•   •
Left Cheek (Center)   Right Cheek (Center)
la reine le veut   *vive la reine*
(the queen wills it)   (long live the queen)

•

Anus
nostalgie de la boue
(nostalgia for the mud)
[homesickness for the gutter]

This is how your lessons go: from clitoris to clitoris, top to bottom. But you must show no accent, speak perfect French, or go back, move backwards, bottom to top.

And she strikes you. She strikes you. With all of her might, she strikes you. With the accuracy of a nun, she strikes you. Ruler on the knuckles, ruler on the palms. Or, if you are very bad, very bad indeed, she paddles your naked ass — all the while you kick and scream, kick and scream.

She once broke a ruler over your ass.

(you can still hear the symphony of its breaking)

And sometimes, sometimes, you will slip on purpose. Sometimes you are very bad.

But, always at the start of class, you place a new ruler atop her desk.

Gift for teacher.

(teacher's pet)

SCHOOLMARM

NE PLUS ULTRA

YOU know that some of us, if only a few of us, are better than the rest of us. Some people are better than others.

You are not thinking of wealth, you are not thinking of genius, you are not even thinking of beauty, you are thinking of those rare individuals, those above wealth, above genius, and yes, above beauty, those above nature, above nurture, those who are above, those who raise themselves above, above their bodies, their minds, biology, society, those who not only set themselves apart from their own nation, but set themselves apart, indeed, carry themselves over, the totality of Man.

Such men, if they are men, are Supermen. Such women, if they are women, are Superwomen. Indeed, they are no longer men or women, but something new, something better, something *over*.

And they are better, they are superior, not by the grace of God (in fact, God would keep them *under*), but, conversely, they are better in spite of grace — in spite, in spite, in spite of all and any other (including, if not especially, the ultimate other, God).

You are, of course, thinking of The Evil Queen.

UEBERMENSCH

OLD NICK

AT breakfast you discuss her oldest friend, her oldest lover, The Devil. The Evil Queen stirs black pepper into her tomato juice, the spoon going around and around, and she tells you secrets:

"Often The Devil has come to me, in the body of a dead man, a man recently hanged. And, being a gentleman, he carries me to my bed chamber, and all the while, I, being a lady, I kiss, I grant long wet kisses, to the expanse of wound that circles his broken neck."

"He has come to me since the onslaught of puberty. And I have never allowed him to be absent longer than a month."

"He has an appetite for menstrual blood. So, I soak my menstrual rags, keeping a special stock of sangria for my favorite guest."

"Of course he has come in many forms: serpent, goat, crow, dog. And always, always, even when a serpent, he is black. And when I really get him going, his cock can exceed the length and width of a man's, indeed, of a very large man's, arm. You would think it comical, a penis that size, defying all gravity, extending from all things, a crow. But you would be wrong. There is nothing more beautiful to behold."

"But, I must confess, I prefer when he comes to me as a woman. Each nipple a crow's beak, cawing, cawing. Each finger, a slender serpent, black, slithering, leaving tiny bites. Cunt hair, coarse as a goat, and often bleeding. And he will bark, bark, like a happy happy bitch, he will bark and bark and bark and bark."

"Broom handle up his ass."

"I am a good witch."

INAMORATA

TITANESS

SHE is tall, yes, but more than that, she is Amazonian. The Evil Queen stands an even 8ft.

She is thin, yes, but more than that, she is skeletal. The Evil Queen weighs an even 100lbs.

Her body is not soft. It is hard.

Her body, hard, so like a statue, is always cold to the touch. Touching The Evil Queen is like touching smooth marble in winter.

You have never seen her shiver.

OSTEOLOGY

DEICIDE

IN ORDER TO KILL GOD,
TO TRULY, TO COMPLETELY, TO FINALLY KILL GOD,
YOU MUST BE WILLING TO LIVE IN ONE OF TWO WORLDS:

A WORLD WITHOUT GOD
OR
A WORLD WHERE YOU ARE GOD

THE FIRST:
A WORLD OF NIETZSCHEAN PLEASURE

THE SECOND:
A WORLD OF BLAKEAN JOY

(DIFFICULT CHOICE)

DEIFY

BIBLIOLATER

SHE is an avid reader. And, more than that, she commits most of what she reads to memory. How does she do it? Simple: She reads every book no less than ten times. And she reads them aloud, slowly, always savoring, savoring the word never read before. She falls in love with any word she meets for the first time. Mysterious, that first reading, like two strangers having sex. And after she knows the word, after she fucks it, it belongs to her. She owns it.

These are the books she read this winter:

Barrett, Francis, *The Magus or Celestial Intelligencer, Being a Complete System of Occult Philosophy* (London, 1801).

[Church, Thomas,] *An Essay Toward Vindicating the Literal Sense of the Demoniacs in the New Testament* (London, 1737).

Farnsworth, Richard, *Witchcraft Cast Out from the Religious Seed and Israel of God* (London, 1655).

More, Henry, *An Antidote Against Atheism* (London, 1653, rev. ed., 1655).

A Narrative of the Suffering and Relief of a Young Girl Strangely Molested by Evil Spirits (Paisley, 1775).

A True Relation of a Very Strange and Wonderful Thing That Was Heard in the Air (London, 1658).

Turner, William, *Complete History of the Most Remarkable Providences* (London, 1697).

You close your eyes when she reads, make believe that she is reading you. Eyes moving from word to word. Tip of finger, wet, turning your pages. She pinches the corner, bending you back to save her place.

DEMONOLOGY

E U N U C H I S M

"I am lowly," you say aloud, while washing The Evil Queen's hair. And it is true, you come from peasant stock.

"The higher that you may climb," she replies (your tiny fingers inching up that thick expanse of black).

"I am common, ordinary, why do you keep me?"

The Evil Queen reaches up from the tub, her wet arms moving in unison, and takes hold of your nipples.

(PINCH) "You are still growing, do not be impatient."
(PINCH) "The blood of every king leads to a commoner."
(PINCH) "Ultimately, it is will, not blood, that will lift the sword."

Rinsing her hair, you think of your penis, floating in that grail, floating in that sangria, in that grail atop her writing desk.

You had not yet reached puberty when she caught you plundering her tomato garden. She took you by the nape, and lifted you up, all-the-way-up, to her face. And she smiled, smiled, that wide dragon smile, her cold breath against you, and spoke: "Back again are you?"

She was impressed. You are the only thief to ever return to her garden. She looks a thief dead in the eye, says a phrase or two in Latin, and then lets the little bandit run for dear life! But you came back.

She has great tomatoes.

Your penis has been in that grail for over 500 years.

HIERODULE

GERMANOPHILE

SHE also teaches you German.

Hence:

ich dien
(I serve)

ein' feste Burg ist unser Gott
(a mighty fortress is our God)

Galgenhumor
(gallows humor)

wunderbar
(wonderful)

German is for the anus of The Evil Queen.

Sometimes you whisper, send tiny vibrations, make the great woman giggle like a little girl.

Sometimes you shout! — sending her into a frenzy, her anus pushing out! out! out! (like a toddler blowing out birthday candles).

But mostly you speak in a firm, sincere tone. And as your lessons proceed, as your vocabulary increases, your lips move deeper and deeper, until, if your studies have gone especially well, your lips disappear altogether, and move in unison, perfect unison, with her asshole.

DER GEIST DER STETS VERNEINT

PAROLE

UP inside her language

                                           rushing toward naked white

      washing

                                       washing

                     washing

                              clitoris after clitoris

            anus after anus

                            page

        after page

after page

                          after page

           tomatoes

                                     burgeoning

                dirty cudgel

gratuitous red

      brimming

                            frothing

                over spill

                              words
          words
                                                  words
awake in the dream of white pages
                                        touching everything
                    everything
          until you
                or she
                                                  awakes
she lifts you from the garden
                                        beats you with a belt
          madness of red
                          barrels and barrels

of red
                          red
                                                  wine
          every finger a scythe
                          hundreds of years to scar
and you swim through her Hell of sangria
                    nine red roses growing from your throat
                    nine red roses growing from your ass

teach me to bark

                              you beg her

          teach

                                   me

                                             to

                              bark

     black cunt

                    a casket

                         soft red velvet inside

               up

                                        up

     up

          you throw up your arms

                    you are torn limb from limb

     limb from limb

                    only please

               please

                         please

                              in her mouth

          in her cunt

                              up her ass
white shoulders
                                        white thighs
            clitoris into thorn

        savage
                                  bone
                                          white
horn against your eunuch middle

                                          your teeth
                your teeth

                              your teeth are on fire

_____

L A N G U E
_____

DE SADE

THE EVIL QUEEN puts the riding crop back into the treasure trove. Like an infant to the crib, she lays the wand down gently. Then she lifts something up, something new, recently wound rope. Oh, how she loves fresh rope, the smell, the coarse texture chafing the skin, your skin. That smell, persistent, sticking to the abrasion. She orders it special from a source in London. Every month, new rope. And it must be red or black, the reddest of red, or the blackest of black. Every month, new rope. You bury the old rope on the last Sunday of every month. You bury it in the rose garden.

Cat-of-nine-tails, the end of each tassel pulled tight into a knot. You have been with her for many years, this is her thirteenth whip.

Leather binding, leather teddy, boots, gloves, masks, nooses, straps, cuffs, prods, and of course, of course, the anal plug. The Evil Queen has everything.

She closes the trunk, pats the lid, kisses the red stripes, kisses your abrasions, your open wounds.

You only play torture chamber on the Sabbath and on holidays.

Not a time of rest, but not a time of work, either.

VON MASOCH

BRUNETTE

"GROTESQUE?" She inquires, one eyebrow moving higher than the other, as you move the comb down to her cunt.

"Monstrous?" As if asking permission, as you move the comb up and under her left armpit.

"Freakish?" This time teasing, as you move the comb from left armpit to right.

You absolutely adore her hair. The hair on her head, of course, beautiful, reaching her ankles. But the hair on her cunt, oh yes, you adore the hair on her cunt even more. Coarse, thick, even blacker than the hair on her head. And long, so long, when you comb it out, reaching down to her white white knees. And her armpits, exquisite. Each roll of hair reaching her hips, if given the comb.

You start at the bottom, slowly moving up, cramming more and more hair into your mouth. You breathe through your noise, soaking, soaking the hair, until all the black is shining, wet. And then you comb, from top to bottom, in slow, even, strokes. Look how it shines like silk in moonlight.

That long expanse of black, your saliva giving it body, the comb smoothing it out.

A waterfall of pubic hair.

TRICHOLOGY

MARIOLATRY

THERE is one room in the castle that contains no less than one thousand statues of The Virgin Mary.

(a large room)

Walking through the room is like walking through a graveyard. Each statue a headstone, a marker for The Dead. The floor, the walls, the ceiling are all painted red. You have never been able to count all the candles. There must be thousands. The candles are black, the dripping wax collects like dung on the floor. Candle after candle, month after month, the heaps of dung pile up. A basin for holy water is in the center of the room. But the basin contains no holy water, it contains only blood, the blood of The Evil Queen. Once a night, when the heavens menstruate at sundown, The Evil Queen kneels at the basin and bleeds her left arm. Drip after drip, night after night, year after year after year, the blood piles up.

The Evil Queen is praying (The Evil Queen is bleeding):

"Pity Mary,
Saint of Rape,
the Lord did Wound thee;
Cursed art thou amongst Women,
and Cursed is the Offense of thy Wound,
Jesus.

Ill Mary,
Sickness of God,
I mourn your Injuries, now
and until the hour of my death.
Amen."

NECROPOLIS

INTERNECINE

SHE is on her third jug of sangria.

You watch her take gulps. Her Eve's Apple, flush, moving up and down, up and down. Thin trails of red, slide off her chin . . . drip . . . drip . . . drip . . .

The clitoris on her throat is swollen.

Her lipstick has smeared on her face, like some great red wound, her mouth a tear, each lip a laceration, her jug of sangria crammed deep into the cut.

Foaming red at the mouth, slurring word after word, you strain to make out her speech:

Tongue is dagger, mouth is sheath
Tongue is dagger, mouth is wound

Fingers once were arms, cut off by a lover
Lover's body, exquisite, gorgeous guillotine

Man's cock is shovel, woman's cunt is grave
Lover's bed is casket, nightfall drops the dirt

Headstone proves to lover, proves that you love
Headstone proves to lover, proves that you are dead

NECROPHILIA

BIBULOUSNESS

YOU are wiping red vomit off the floor. The stench is overwhelming. But slowly, slowly, wipe after wipe, you find yourself smiling, growing not just accustomed to the stench, to the reeking gore, but growing to like it. There is something familiar, something comfortable, almost, almost . . . nostalgic.

Last night was the first time you ever carried The Evil Queen to her bed (usually she carries you). She was surprisingly light. The water buckets would seem to weigh more. You carried her in your arms, walking that long hall to her bed chamber, you undressed her, and put her to bed.

You did not even mind that she puked on you.

There was something intimate about the act, the act of her vomiting on you. All that gore, all that stench, came from deep, deep, deep within The Evil Queen. A penis could never reach that depth. You had on you the muck of her being, the absolute foulest of her core.

Red red secrets. Red red shames.

She passed out before she puked. It could be your own little secret.

There, you are done cleaning. But wait, you hear her calling. She is calling for more sangria.

EMETOPHILIA

P E D A G O G Y

WHAT YOU ARE LEARNING FROM THE EVIL QUEEN:

LATIN

FRENCH

GERMAN

LATIN	FRENCH	GERMAN
Mystagogue	Pedagogue	Apologue
Metaphor	Paramour	Armature
Mystery	Puberty	Authority
(Blood)	(Flesh)	(Bone)
(Ink)	(Pages)	(Binding)

M Y S T A G O G Y

NEPHILIM

YOU are thinking of the beauty of The Evil Queen. Not the innocent, not the untouched, not the clean beauty of the virgin. Oh no, nothing so boring, nothing so tame as that. No, you are thinking of the experienced, the touched, the outright filthy beauty of the whore.

The true difference between the virgin and the whore, theological nonsense put aside, is that the act of sex robs the virgin of her power, where as the same act, acted out over and over and over again, only adds to the power of the whore. Put another way: the virgin can only lose power, the whore can only gain it.

The Evil Queen has no doubt been a whore for a very long time. Most women have one clitoris, The Evil Queen has ten. You almost feel, almost, that The Evil Queen was the first whore — but that would be absurd.

Last night she read to you from the books Genesis, Numbers, and Deuteronomy. You where shocked to learn that a race of giants had long ago walked the earth. The Sons of God (angels?), came down from Heaven and were wedded to human women — the so-called Daughters of Man. These divine-human marriages produced giants! You found this all very interesting.

And more, The Evil Queen had information about these giants, information not to be found in The Old Testament. On three separate occasions, she put down the Bible, put you on her lap, and recounted tales (could they have only been tales?), on the lives of these giants from before The Flood. Life *before* The Flood. She used proper names when she told the tales, the proper names of the giants, and, what is more, she knew . . .

ANTEDILUVIAN

MIRACLE PLAY

SHE is loved by the local actors. Amateur and professional alike. When the actors are out of work (and they are often out of work), she sponsors a play. There is a small theater on the castle compound. Small it may be, but it is stocked full of supplies: set equipment, costumes, makeup, whatever one would need to put on a splendid play. And she pays the actors, often twice what they make at the local theater. They perform religious drama.

She has written several scripts. These are the only plays to be performed on her stage. The Evil Queen provides the text, the actors provide the performance. She has a collection of medieval religious plays. These she uses as the model, as the bones, but she adds her own touch, her own flesh, to complete the text. She transforms pious propaganda into devilish debauchery. Dogma into drama. The actors love it. And her favorite, of course, is The Passion of Christ. But she also enjoys the reenactment of torturing saints. Martyrdom makes for great scenes on the stage.

You and The Evil Queen are the only audience. First you rub the clitoris on her nape, slowly following the knobs that divide the center of her back, glide your fingertips down her spine. Then you creep your hand under the hem of her gown, make your way over her thighs, descend to that hairy cunt. You rub her slowly as the drama proceeds, move your middle finger in those little circles, in those little Os. Soon you are working both her front and back, one finger atop her cunt, one finger up her ass.

The Romans are whipping Jesus, you hear her whisper *faster*. The Romans are pushing down that crown of thorns, you hear her whisper *faster*. The Romans are nailing, nailing, nailing Jesus to The Cross, you hear her whisper   *faster*   *faster*   *faster*.

MYSTERY PLAY

AMOUR PROPRE

The self-approval, the self-assurance, the self-regard of The Evil Queen:
"Oh I never! Oh I never! Oh I never grow tired of being The Evil
Queen!"

(Arrogance)

(Aggression)

(Autonomy)

HAUTEUR

BILLET-DOUX

DEAREST MEPHISTOPHELES:

The Evil Queen has not only departed the castle compound, as rare as that may be, but she has left the country for no less than three weeks. This has, as you yourself can well imagine, provided me with ample time to thoroughly snoop through all The Evil Queen's confidential files (as was no doubt her intent). Hence, I now possess your address.

It was quite the adventure. Going from hall to hall, from room to room, checking every inch of the castle, taking my time. I found no less than thirteen secret doors, twenty secret panels, and sixty-six human skeletons. Normally, she watches me as I clean, so I have not had the privacy to snoop. She had something hidden under every statue of The Virgin Mary. I put everything back in its place (after making copies of everything of interest to me).

I, of course, am the eunuch that cares for her estate. I am the maid, the cook, the butler, the groundskeeper, and the gardener all rolled into one (well, to be honest, I am the assistant gardener, she is obsessed with the care, no, with the perfection, of her rosery and tomato patches). Anyway, I am her servant. She has left England to attend a week-long conference on Transcendentalism in New York. She also plans to make love to the American writer Edgar Allan Poe (i.e., she plans to murder him).

As you well know, The Evil Queen grows more and more depressed the closer we approach the new century. She often sits atop her bed, through all hours of the night, placing tarot card after tarot card in the pattern of The Cross. She is becoming something of a nocturnal recluse, almost cadaveric, her nudity aglow against the candle light, like some statue of a saint in a dark gothic church. She is sleeping less and less each night. She is starting to depress me. I am no longer allowed to touch her after midnight. She is even beginning to rush my lessons. I can sense the urgency in her, her sense that time is running out.

One would assume that it must make her more depressed, always getting the same tarot reading, over and over, night after night, but somehow the consistency comforts her (I am not sure I understand the paradox).

The night before she left for New York, The Evil Queen sat me on her lap, took my little hands to her lips, kissed, and spoke thus: "The Industrial Revolution is fast killing my kind. The future of The Occident is bleak. In the century to come, German will go too far, French will not go far enough, and Latin, sacred Latin, will cease to be employed by the religious. Indeed, few will be religious. Europe, finally, after her long struggle, will be civilized. I will have no place."

She was, of course, drunk when she told me this.

My reason for writing you is specific. I must replace The Evil Queen. I need your help. I cannot do it without you. You granted power to The Evil Queen on her first menstruation, you will grant power to me on my first erection. She has told me that my education is nearing its completion (perhaps only forty or so years to go). I believe that she is telling me the truth when she says that the next century will have no place for her. I also believe that I must take her place. Evil must continue, despite modernism, despite the death of God (and, by default, the death of you).

My room is behind the thirteenth door on the left, west wing, just six rooms down from the castle library. I will keep both my door and window unlocked. After midnight, The Evil Queen has nothing to do with me. We will have no interruptions. I look forward to your guidance.

Yours Faithfully,
THE EUNUCH

P.S. How did The Evil Queen have tomatoes before the 16th century?

T R Y S T

FIDUS ACHATES

MEPHISTOPHELES:

MOST BELOVED F(R)IEND TO BOTH QUEEN AND EUNUCH

PEDERAST

AMBROSIA

ONCE every fifty-five years, at the crack of dawn, The Evil Queen has a special meal brought before her. For two weeks preceding the meal, you and The Evil Queen fast, a true fast, not even taking water. As the days proceed, the pain increases, and as the pain increases, delirium slowly sets in. Like a specter creeping, creeping up to haunt your head, nightmares, visions, voices. She tells you that the first time is always the worst. And you believe her, she seems hardly troubled at all.

The special cook is summoned. He cooks the entire day leading up to dawn. He rings the bell, then disappears.

They are beautiful, those mounds of flesh, those heaps of meat. Normally, The Evil Queen has impeccable manners. Her table etiquette is unparalleled. But not for this meal. This meal she will eat with her hands.

You and The Evil Queen are naked. Both of you are rolling on the meat, like happy dogs scratching their backs, you are rolling, rolling on the meat. Rolling becomes wrestling, wrestling atop heaps of wet flesh, you are slapping each other with hunks of dripping meat. She overpowers you, holds your small arms behind your back, giggles in your ear, then forces your face down, down, deep into it. You slip free, grab a chunk, cram it into her face. She pushes you on your stomach, throws meat on your back, eats like a hungry animal, eating through the meat to get to you. Now she is feeding you, now you are feeding her. White fingers smear blood on white bodies. When the meat is gone you both begin to bite each other.

It was the best meat you ever tasted. You only wish that you knew, that you knew who the men were, the men who you had eaten.

A N T H R O P O P H A G U S

AUTOMATIC WRITING

SHE tells you that sometimes, sometimes, the pen just writes by it-self. Or, if it is not the pen, then perhaps it is her hand, her left hand writing, writing without her, or perhaps, despite her. Sometimes she just watches the ink swim across the page, letters forming words, the words gliding into sentences, into paragraphs. Sometimes she sits down to her writing desk, full after a large breakfast, only to find herself hungry, hungry for dinner. No memory of the day.

She calls it Automatic Writing.

This writing is always in Latin.

This Latin is always in the form of letters, letters from a stranger to The Evil Queen.

(no return address)

She does not know if she is blessed, possessed, or both. And she does not care. Whose ever writing it is, whatever its origin, it is beautiful.

She has read every classic in the Latin language, this Latin is better.

The strange thing, and a primitive thing it is, is that she burns everything she writes. Everything she writes, she keeps for 100 years, then burns it.

"Do not worry," she tells you, setting those stacks of paper ablaze, "they always come back, the important part is the writing."

EPISTLE

AMOUR

IT would be the last time Merlin would visit the castle, the last time that he would ever speak to The Evil Queen. They were old friends, long trading secrets, long keeping a friendly rivalry. But she had eventually won. She no longer needed him.

He was quite upset.

He believed that she had gone too far. She believed that she had not gone far enough.

(she meant to go further)

You could hear them screaming, screaming in French, screaming from all the way down the corridor. You could make out some of what they were saying. Peeking out from behind a pillar, you strained to listen, but dared not move.

Merlin:
(shaking his bony finger in her face) "! ! ! . . . j'accuse . . . ! ! !"

[I accuse]

The Evil Queen:
"! ! ! . . . autres temps, autres moeures . . . ! ! !"

[other times, other customs]

M:
(knocking the crown off her head)
"! ! ! . . . j'accuse . . . ! ! !"

[I accuse]

Q:
(slapping him across the face)
"! ! ! . . . tant mieux . . . ! ! !"

[so much the better]

M:
(slapping her back)
"! ! ! . . tant pis . . . ! ! !"

[so much the worse]

Q:

"! ! ! le coeur a ses raisons que la raison ne connait point ! ! !"

[the heart has its reasons that reason knows nothing of]

M:

(he is pulling hard on her arm)

! ! ! . . . acte gratuit . . . ! ! !"

[gratuitous impulsive act]

Q:

(in-between laughing)

"! ! ! . . . tout bien ou rien . . . ! ! !"

[everything well (done) or nothing (attempted)]

M:

(his face growing redder and redder)

"! ! ! . . . en ami . . . ! ! !"

[as a friend]

Q:

(laughing, mocking, voice even louder)

"! ? ! . . . en ami . . . ? ! ?"

[(?) as a friend(?)]

M:
(pleading, pleading)
"! ! ! . . . crise de conscience . . . ! ! !"

[crisis of conscience]

Q:
(still mocking, still laughing)
"! ! ! . . . sans doute . . . ! ! !"

[without doubt]

M:
(turns his back, wipes a tear, heads for door)
"! ! ! bonsoir ! ! !"

[good evening]

Q:
(she pulls a dagger from her gown, grabs the old man by his gray hair, kicks his feet out from under him, throws his body to the floor, and says, while stabbing, stabbing, stabbing him over and over and over again)
"! ! ! au contraire ! ! !"

[on the contrary]

ANNULMENT

A P O S T A S Y

THE HERESIES OF THE PAST ARE THE ORTHODOXIES OF THE PRESENT. THE HERESIES OF THE PRESENT ARE THE ORTHODOXIES OF THE FUTURE. THE FOUNDERS AND REFORMERS OF TRUE RELIGION WERE FIRST AND FOREMOST HERETICS (JESUS, MUHAMMAD, LUTHER). HERESY IS ORTHODOXY IN DISGUISE. ORTHODOXY IS HERESY IN DISGUISE. A THEOLOGICAL MOBIUS STRIP. THE PARADOX CONFUSES YOU: AGNOSTICISM (BEST TO LEAVE THE PARADOX TO OTHERS). THERE IS NO PARADOX: SECTARIANISM (NO PARADOX FOR THE TRUE BELIEVER). THE PARADOX IS IRRELEVANT: SECULARISM (THE PARADOX HAS NO BEARING ON MY REAL LIFE). THE PARADOX IS TRUE: UNITARIANISM (ALL IN GOOD TIME). CUT THE STRIP IN HALF: ATHEISM (THE PARADOX IS A FAKE).

H E T E R O D O X Y

FUCK

CUNT, subs. (common). —— The female pudendum; Latin cunnus. A language word, but vulgar in usage. Diminutives of varying degrees are CUNNICLE, CUNNIKIN, CUNTKIN, CUNTLET, CUNNY. Derivatives, the result of an obvious play upon words (old), are CUNNY-CATCHER and CUNNY-BURROW FERRET (Urquhart), for which see CREAM-STICK; CUNNY-HUNTER = a whoremonger; and CUNNY-SKIN (Durfey), for which see FLEECE. For synonyms, see MONOSYLLABLE.

1383. CHAUCER, *The Miller's Tale.* Full prively he caught her by the QUEINT, And sayde Ywis but if I have my will, For derne love of thee, lemman, I spill.

1622. FLETCHER, *Spanish Curate.* They write sunt with a C, which is abominable.

1647-80. ROCHESTER, *The Royal Angler.* However weak and slender in the string, Bait it with CUNT, and it will hold a king.

1768. STERNE, *The Sentimental Journey.* So that, when I stretched out my hand, I caught hold of the Fille-de-chambre's ——.

FUCK, subs. (venery). —— 1. An act of coition. For synonyms, see GREENS.

2. (venery). —— The Seminal fluid. For synonyms, see CREAM.

Verb (common). —— To copulate. For synonysms, see GREENS and RIDE.

c.1540. DAVID LYNDSAY. *'Flyting with King James.'* Aye FUKKAND like ane furious fornicator.

1568. CLERK, *Bannatyne MSS.,* Hunterian Soc. Publication, p. 298. He clappit fast, he kist, he chukkit, As with the glaikkis he wer ourgane; Yit be his feiris he waid haif FUKKIT.

1568. Anonymous, *Bannatyne MSS.,* Hunterian Soc. Publication, p. 399. 'In somer when flouris will smell.' Allace! said sch, my awin sweit thing, Your courtly FUKKING garis me fling, Ye wirk sae weill.

1598. FLORIO, *A Worlde of Wordes,* Fottere. To jape; to sarde, to FUCKE; to swive; to occupy.

1620. PEICY, *Folio MSS.,* p.459 [Hales and Furnivall, 1867.] A mighty mind to clipp, kisse, and to FFUCK her.

1647-80. ROCHESTER, *'Written under Nelly's Picture.'* Her father FUCKED them right together.

1683. EARL OF DORSRET, *'A Faithful Cataloque.'* From St. Jame's to the land of Thule, There's not a whore who F——S so like a mule.

c. 1716-1746, ROBERTSON of Struan, *Poems*, p. 256. But she gave proof that she could F——K, Or she is damnably bely'd.

1728. BAILEY, *English Dict.*, S.V. FUCK . . . Feminam subigitare.

1728. GROSE, *Vulg. Tongue.* F——-K, to copulate.

c. 1790 (?). BURNS. *Merry Muses.* And yet misca's a poor thing That FUCKS for its bread.

[From J. S. Farmer's *Slang and its Analogues* — your favorite book]

C U N T

H O M U N C U L U S

YOU do not regret being a dwarf.

That you are a dwarf, that you are the smallest man The Evil Queen has ever seen, pleases her. And you are even short for a dwarf. You stand an even 1ft. You are the tiniest of men.

You and The Evil Queen are playing "Hide-and-Seek." It is Saturday, game day, the day set aside for play. Sometimes you play "Leprechaun-and-Gold," sometimes "Spider-and-Fly." All of these games, and there are many, involve one of you hiding, and one of you seeking. Right now you are hiding in the sugar jar.

You are eating the sugar, cramming the pretty white into your mouth, handful after handful, being a bad bad boy. You are licking your pudgy fingers, sucking off the sweet.

She finds you, your face a sticky mess, wet white globs falling from your mouth as you beg her not to spank you. Five white spears, the tips blood-red, are thrown into the sugar jar. She grabs you.

She has a special comb, primitive designs on antique ivory, it is her spanking comb.

(WHACK) You are crying out that you will never do it again!
(WHACK) You are telling her it is your last time, you promise!
(WHACK) You are kicking and screaming, begging her to stop!

(WHACK - WHACK - WHACK)

This is an anniversary spanking. It is the 100th time she has caught you in the sugar jar.

FERULE

T R A N S C R I B E

SHE wrote a poem tonight. All on her own, no help from Automatic Writing. She wrote it in her favorite language, Latin.

And after she wrote it, she went for a horseback ride. She loves that horse, the one she named Nightmare. She only rides her nude, bare-back, at night. She pushes that horse, pushes her hard. White legs kicking black hide, white hands pulling black mane. Sometimes the horse collapses, exhausted, unable to run on, and she will kiss Nightmare's forehead, covering her face with the horse's sweat.

You sneak into her bed chamber, copy the poem, bring the copy back to your room. You read it over, get an idea.

Ode To The Strange Woman

"Thine eyes shall behold strange woman, and thine heart shall utter perverse things." (Proverbs 23:33)

> Long have kings quilled words to daunt
> their countries' sons' wayfaring want;
> but all men youthful must beseech
> the one aside her door to preach.
>
> For smoother than oil anointed in dark
> her honeycomb mouth whispers softly embark;
> then ravenous kisses as a monk whip self sent
> bestow orchid emblems as night's ornament.
>
> And besmeared purpled eyelids all whorish do blink
> as stars in dark heaven through twilight fain wink;
> thus Lilith's eyelashes like butterflies fall
> for gathered lilies are the perfumed solace pall.

You like the poem. Your very first translation. You even made it rhyme. You are so proud of yourself. Little translator. You are growing up. Best to hide it before she gets back.

STRANGE WOMAN

WHORE

NOTORIOUS WHORES:
see Mary Magdalene,
empress Theodora,
St. Helena

WHORE AS RELIGIOUS PROFESSION:
see *devadasis* (Hindu),
ghazye (Egyptian),
zonah (Hebrew)

CRITICAL STUDY ON THE WHORE:
see Lorenzo Valla's *De Voluptate*

PATRON SAINTS OF THE WHORE:
see St. Aphra,
St. Maudline

VIEWS OF ST. THOMAS AQUINAS:
"lawful immorality"

FAMOUS WHOREHOUSES:
see Temple of Juno Sospita,
the Parthenon

WHOREDOM

ASSHOLE

YOU are remembering the first time you licked her asshole.

She came back from the privy, you washed her anus. Washed it all clean. "But how can I know it is clean, I mean, how can I know for certain?" She was teasing you, baiting you.

And without her even asking, you kissed it. Just a little peck, like kissing a parent's cheek, no tongue. In its own way, it was innocent.

She became silent, began moving slowly, slowly lowering her head to the floor, slowly rising her white ass into the air. Her asshole became the mouth of a beast, a sphinx, something horrible, something incredible, something hungry, something to be fed.

Just your lips at first, little kisses. Small lips, soft, slow, kissing. But soon you set your tiny tongue free. Out it goes, serpentine, pink, wet, sliding, sliding, side to side, top to bottom, around and around and around. And soon you are stabbing, stabbing, stabbing with that tiny tongue, struggling to break through, struggling to stab her through and through, struggling, struggling, struggling to break her open.

She spreads her legs far apart, stretches her white arms like Christ across the castle floor. Her asshole is moving, straining to speak, pushing, like lips, pushing out. You are a miner, throwing your tiny shovel, throwing your tiny pink shovel with all you have got.

You fucked that magnificent asshole with your tongue.

That was so long ago.

(you miss her asshole most of all)

A N I L I N G U S

CAPUT

SHE told you many bedtime stories. Your favorite stories were always of the virgin martyrs, those beautiful women, beheaded. They always chose decapitation. Not one betrayed her lover.

St. Agnes (d. middle or end the 3rd century) — Synopsis: This little tease was only twelve years old when her strut could no longer be ignored by the pagan son of the Prefect of Rome. This poor boy, haunted by her beauty (a beauty never touched), confessed to his daddy that he had to have her. His daddy, himself a healthy pagan, well understood. The boy, guided by the advice of his daddy, began courting her with promises, moved soon to threats, and ended by begging his daddy to arrest her, which he did for his loving son. The Prefect had the little tease arrested, stripped naked, and sent her post haste to his favorite brothel. But Jesus Christ would not have his lover seen by another man. The hair atop her head, accompanied by the hair from under each armpit, and the hair atop her virgin cunt, grew by a miracle to cover the nudity of his young lover. Much fuss was made over the fact that Agnes could not be burned by the flames that rose from her pyre. This so angered the Prefect, who wanted so very much to watch that little tease go up in smoke, that he ordered her head cut off. Which was done.

St. Barbara (d. about 235) — <u>Synopsis</u>: This little tease, as much loved by her father as by Jesus Christ, was shut up in a high tower to keep her away from men. It was a beautiful tower, having two windows, and was surrounded by a magnificent garden. Her loving father wanted to keep his sweet daughter all to himself. But her father was good enough to send for philosophers, orators, and poets to educate his special little girl. She was indifferent to the lessons of wisdom provided by her heathen teachers and snuck out in spirit to flirt with Christ. She so fell in love with Christ that she persuaded some workmen, in her father's absence, to add a third window to the tower. The third window, of course, made her father's tower Christ's. The two windows of her father, two windows symbolic of two male human eyes, became three windows, became three windows symbolic of the Christian Trinity. Her father was so hurt by his daughter's betrayal, by her dishonor to him, that he handed the little tease over to the Roman authorities. There she was tortured. When it came time to finally put the Christian to death, her father came forward and asked if he may have the honor of killing her. He was granted the honor. He cut her head clean off with one blow from his axe.

St. Catherine of Alexandria (d. early 4th century [?]) —
<u>Synopsis</u>: From very early in life this little tease showed great
potential for scholarship. But she would come to forsake her
gift and flirt with Christ. Soon after this virgin became queen,
she converted to Christianity. The emperor Maxentius desired
to have her. He thought that by sending fifty philosophers, by
sending fifty of his finest thinkers to discuss the matter of her
"heavenly groom," that he could show her the folly of her
ways and marry her. He had no such luck. Not only did the
fifty philosophers not convince her, but she converted them
to Christianity! The emperor had the fifty men put to death.
He then constructed a spiked wheel designed to tear the little
tease apart. But Christ denied the spiked wheel to tear apart
little Catherine. Christ destroyed the spiked wheel with a bolt
of lightning. The emperor was left solely to have her beheaded. Which he did.

You loved those stories of the virgin martyrs, those decapitations.
Why so special, decapitation? Why could Christ not prevent it?

DECOLLATION

T R A V A I L

SHE taught you to take responsibility.

She taught you to take responsibility for your pain.

"It is your pain," she would say, often after spanking you. "It is your pain, all yours, learn to treasure it."

Your ass tomato-red.

At first you did not understand. You were too young, you thought that pain came to you, like a gift. But you grew up, just like she said you would, and you grew to understand that pain was not given, was not passive, but was taken, was active.

Pain is loot not boon.

And once one has it, and you learned to hoard it, once one under-stands that pain can never be taken back, it becomes treasure, becomes wealth, the only thing stolen that can never be stolen back.

The perfect crime.

Pain can never be removed. Pain can never be returned. Too many confuse paining others with returning pain. Paining others is a para-dox: the burglar convincing the householder that nothing is out of place. This is the child's mistake. Thinking that something as pro-found as pain, something as permanent, can be shared, can be traded back and forth, like some nursery school novelty. Nonsense.

Pain cannot be granted. It can be offered, yes, one may leave the gate unlocked, but more often than not it is simply taken.

Fools believe that pain is not stolen.

The wise know full well what plunder they possess.

Each pain a brick, a brick used to build, to build one up. Even if they are the bricks of a dungeon, the bricks of a torture chamber, cold stonework going down, down, going deep down into the dark — or, better, *especially* if.

You must never forget that it was you who returned to The Evil Queen's tomato garden.

SAPIENCE

INHUMATION

YOU are opening the cunt of The Evil Queen. Your two dwarf hands, shaking, your ten pudgy fingers, trembling, trembling, you are pulling with all your might to open The Evil Queen. Your tiny arms hurt, your little muscles ache, it takes all that you have to sustain the opening.

She is telling you you are strong, so strong. Like Samson, like Hercules.

She grabs you by the legs and forces you in.

Like a knife, like a dagger, your body is a weapon, she is stabbing, stabbing, she is attacking her cunt. Her cunt, her cunt, is a glorious wound.

It is wet. It is dark. The pressure of collapsing flesh is all around you. Wet-Darkness. Dark-Wetness. The horror of sodden meat, crushing you, in pauses — tighten, release, tighten, release. You are inside a terrible mouth. It is chewing, it is smashing, it is gobbling, gobbling, it is gobbling you up.

You are being buried, buried alive.

Suffocating, your body is thrown into spasms. The more you thrash, the more you panic, the more she forces you, the harder she pushes, and faster, faster, her fingers bruising your legs, her cunt a gaping wound, slimy, sticky, you are going deeper and deeper, you believe you are going to die.

Thickness all around you, like snot, like bile. Thick, salty, you are choking, choking, the gore is in your mouth.

VIVISEPULTURE

HARUSPEX

The psychology of The Evil Queen: (she is yelling) "Hope? Dream? Aspire? I will have none of it! If I have character, if I have will, then I need never hope! Life will not come to me, I must call it, take it, if need be, enslave it, but whatever I do, I must go to it! I must grab it! And once I have it, once it is mine, I keep it, I hide it, I do what I must, I never give it up, it is mine!" The Evil Queen is complete.

Completion is a matter of character, a matter of will.

Black Magic in the life of The Evil Queen: She is fond of crows. She often goes out onto the lawn, nude, barefoot atop the dew damp grass. She dances for a while, slow, always slow, a smile on her face. She will twirl, twirl, a skeleton ballerina twirling toward the middle of the lawn. She will fall on her back, spread her legs, roll her arms out like Christ, and caw, caw, caw like a crow. And they come, they descend. One by one, crow by crow, the green green grass becomes black black plumage. First they are shy, just stand on the grass, still. But then they all begin to move, move toward the center of the lawn, move toward her. Soon they are all around her, circling, but afraid to touch. But one touches her, then two, soon they are all climbing on top of her. She will lie there for hours, under that blanket of crows. Motionless white skin under moving black feathers. The birds appear so peaceful, so tame.

Then they all fly upward, all in a panic, bumping into one another, accompanied by shrieks, by caws of alarm. She returns to the castle with a dead crow in her mouth. She spits, the bird drops to the floor. She gets down on her hands and knees, puts one palm up, you hand her the knife. She slices it down the middle, spreads it wide open, pulls out the entrails, and tells you the future.

Black Magic is a matter of character, a matter of will.

FAIT ACCOMPLI

AUT CAESAR AUT NULLUS

YOU and The Evil Queen are playing "Hide-and-Seek."

She is hiding. You are seeking.

She is not in the dungeon. She is not in the torture chamber. She is not in the alchemy lab. She is not in the wine cellar. She is not in the armory. She is not in the throne room. She is not in her bed chamber. She is not in your bed chamber. She is not in the library. She is not in the privy. Wait . . . think . . . you have not yet checked the aviary.

100 cages. 100 crows.

She has sliced their tongues in two. She has taught them Latin. Right now they are all screaming. Their sliced tongues slipping in and out, playing "peek-a-boo" from behind their beaks. They are screaming in Latin. It is almost unbearable. You step in.

AUT CAESAR AUT NIHIL

AUT CAESAR AUT NULLUS

AUT CAESAR AUT NIHIL

AUT CAESAR AUT NULLUS

She has let them out of their cages. They are flying in a panic throughout the room. Black feathers are falling to the floor. She sneaks up behind you, puts her hands over your eyes, and shouts: "Guess Who?"

Still shouting: "Guess Who You Are? Guess Who You Want To Be?"

AUT CAESAR AUT NIHIL

DIRGE

I no longer pour your red red wine
caw caw caw
I no longer wash your white white ass
caw caw caw
Evil Queen, I will miss your wine
Evil Queen, I will miss your ass
Evil Queen
Evil Queen
caw   caw   caw

ELEGY

C O R V U S

RAVEN/CROW [notebook, p.3]:

Long long ago, there was a beautiful maiden named Coronis. She was
a mere mortal, but her beauty was so great that the god Apollo fell in
love with her.

Indeed, Apollo loved her more than any other — including any god.

But Coronis did not return the god's love. The beautiful maiden
loved another — she loved a mere mortal.

Coronis often met her true beloved in secret. She believed she could
fool Apollo. She believed she could keep the truth of her true love
hidden from the god who showered her with divine affection. But
she was the fool to believe that she could deceive the god who loved
her.

The news of her unfaithfulness was brought to Apollo by his faithful bird, the raven.

The raven, then a bird of pure white plumage, flew at once to his god to tell of her trickery.

But the news of her betrayal so consumed Apollo, that, in a fit of anger, he exacted his wrath upon the one closest to him — his loyal raven.

The raven, that white white bird, so clean, so pure, was turned black, made filthy, defiled. To this day the raven is still a cursed creature, flying on black black wings, punished for being faithful, still cursed by the complete injustice of an angry god.

Of course the beautiful Coronis was promptly put to a painful death.

"And these are they which ye shall have in abomination among the fowls; they shall not be eaten, they are an abomination: . . . Every raven after his kind"
(Leviticus 11:13-15)

RAVEN/CROW [notebook, p. 9]:

Two ravens perch atop the shoulders of a god — Odin. Odin, father of war, supreme god, creator of the world, sends these black creatures out each morning to fly over the earth. They bring back to their god all the news of the world.

One raven is Huginn (Thought).

One raven is Muninn (Memory).

The fear of Huginn is great indeed — but the fear of Muninn is even greater. More than one man has surveyed the sky before taking counsel with his fellow man (or cleaving his axe into him).

Odin thinks long and hard on all that Huginn and Muninn bring him. Odin knows that the day of doom is coming. He can do his best to postpone it, but he knows it must eventually come.

He knows that he too must die.

"And the ravens brought him bread and flesh in the morning,
and bread and flesh in the evening"
(I Kings 17:06)

RAVEN/CROW [notebook, p. 18]:

Allah sends a raven to show Cain how to hide the shame of his murdered brother Abel. The raven descends, lands next to the corpse, and scratches the earth.

Cain is to act in kind if he wishes to conceal his slain brother.

But Cain cannot duplicate the despicable act — he cannot bury his brother Abel. The raven's deed is too low.

Cain throws Abel over his shoulder. He wanders through the wasteland, brother carrying dead brother, under the ardent sheen of the desert sun. Days upon days, weeks upon weeks, Cain trudges over the sand. All the while Abel, a ragged heap of stinking death, decomposes more and more.

The reeking gore that is his brother Abel is astonishing in its brutal horror.

Shame swells up in the heart of Cain. Remorse consumes him. From deep deep inside, he pleads for forgiveness. He utters his request, letting his woe soar high high, up up to heaven. Allah knows he is truly sorry.

Allah, in His infinite mercy, allows Cain to repent.

"Who provideth for the raven his food? when his young
ones cry unto God, they wander for lack of meat"
(Job 38:41)

RAVEN/CROW [notebook, p. 54]:

From a wheat field rises a flock of crows. The crows take three paths:
one path leads to the center of the field, another path leads to the
right of the field, another path leads to the left. There are also two
clouds in the sky.

Vincent van Gogh, writing about his last painting, *Wheat Field with
Crows*, had this to say: "They are immense stretches of wheat under
troubled skies, and I did not have to strain in order to seek to express
sadness."

And the great painter inserted these two words between the lines:
"extreme solitude."

Vincent van Gogh painted his work in the very wheat field where he
took his own life.

[last entry in notebook — translated from Latin]

RAVEN HEAD

Raven head, whose black beak rarely sweetly sings,
       but who nightly caws the notes of horror;
sable monstrosity with outstretched wings,
       who has forever been my secret mirror.

Raven head, who from under the rose,
       peers out beneath that black mourning cowl;
blood-wafer from my mouth who arose,
       to meet with light a doleful howl.

Raven head, that ebony Godhead token,
       whose pierced claws trickle cold down the tree;
emblem of mournful remembrance unspoken,
       whose black baptismal screams seeketh me.

Raven head, both my mortician and my mother,
       who lifts my cradle up with the new eastern dawn;

then drops my casket under the western night's smother,
       and surrenders no flowers to my carcass — her spawn.

CAPUT CORVI

NEOLOGISM

PORNOLEXICOLOGY *noun* [*porno* (harlot) + *lexis* (word, speech)] (ca. 1910) 1 *general* : a branch of linguistics concerned with the signification and application of erotic and *especially* obscene words 2 *specific* : a branch of linguistics concerned with the signification and application of erotic and *especially* obscene words as a means to decipher the lewdness of Occidentalism —- see PORNOLEXICOLOGIST *noun*

GONOCENTRIC *adjective* [*gonos* (procreation, seed) + *kentron* (center)] (ca. 1910) 1a *general* : having sex as a central interest b *specific* : having one's own sexual drive as a central interest 2: characterized by or based on the attitude that sex is the central motive of behavior (e.g., Darwinism, Freudianism) — see GONOCENTRISM *noun*

THEOPHILIA *noun* [*theo* (god) + *philia* (friendship), fr. *philos* (dear)] (ca. 1910) 1 : unusual admiration and affection for God (e.g., excessive worship of God; or — more important — the persistent feeling of being in the presence of a loving God) 2a *general* : obsession with and *usually* (unconscious) erotic interest in God b *specific* : sexual perversion in which God is the preferred sexual object —see THEOPHILIAC *noun*, see THEOPHILE *noun*

NOMENCLATURE

QUEENSHIP

"Which king?"

(you are combing her hair)

"Which king have I sat beside?"

(white white comb combing black black hair)

"Which king has made me Queen?"

(her hair has many tangled knots)

"Does not every Queen need a king?"

(you are tugging, tugging, tugging on the knots)

"Was it Akhenaton, king of Egypt, who started the Aton cult? Was it Ashurbanipal, last of *the Great* kings of Assyria? Was it Xerxes I, *the Great* king of Persia? Was it Alexander III of Macedon, *the Great* king? Was it Asoka, king of Magadha? Was it Jugurtha, king of Numidia? Was it Herod, *the Great* Roman king of Judea, who ordered the massacre of the Innocents? Was it Alaric, Visigoth king, conqueror of Rome? Was it Attila, the *Scourge of God*, king of the Huns, who died of overindulgence at his wedding feast? Was it Chlodwig, king of the Salian Franks? Was it Theodoric, *the Great* king of Ostrogoths? Was it Charlemagne, Charles the Great, Frankish king, emperor of the West? Was it Alfred, *the Great* king of Wessex? Was it Brian, king of Ireland? Was it Edmund, *Ironside*, king of the English? Was it Baldwin I, *brother of Godfrey of Bouillon*, king of Jerusalem? Was it Lothair II, king of Germany, Holy Roman emperor? Was it Robert I, *the Bruce*, king of Scotland? Was it John I, *the Great* king of Portugal? Was it Atahaullpa, the last Inca king of Peru? Was it Kamehameha, *the Great* king of Hawaii? Or was it Christophe, king of Haiti?"

"No, none of these kings made me Queen."

"Indeed, truth be known, I have had the pleasure of rejecting every one of them."

"The more kings I reject, the greater my pleasure."

"I do not mean to boast, but I have had the pleasure of rejecting a great many kings. I have rejected two kings named Umberto, two kings named William, three kings named Artaxerxes, three kings named Cleomenes, three kings named Darius, three kings named Richard, four kings named Ferdinand, four kings named Thutmose, five kings named Harold, five kings named Olaf, six kings named Afonso, six kings named James, seven kings named Frederick, nine kings named Edward, eleven kings named Ramses, twelve kings named Charles, twelve kings named Henry, twelve kings named Philip, thirteen kings named Antiochus, fifteen kings named Ptolemy, and eighteen kings named Louis."

"I have lost count of the number of kings I have rejected. But I have rejected every one."

"I have rejected great kings and small kings alike."

"I have rejected every last one."

"I rejected the first king and I will reject the last."

(all the tangles are out of her hair)

"No pleasure is greater than rejecting the great."

(you save every strand of her discarded hair)

"And my greatest pleasure, oh yes, yes, my greatest pleasure, my greatest pleasure comes from rejecting the King of Kings — it is possible to reject that king every day."   Whispering: *"And I do."*

(you keep dolls under your pillow that you make from her hair)

QUEEN REGNANT

CORPUS DELICTI

SHE is in the cemetery. The cemetery that takes up the western most part of the castle compound. There are many graves. Each grave has a headstone. Each headstone has a heading. Name. Date of birth. Date of death. No strangers are buried in the cemetery. The Evil Queen knew every one.

The cemetery is the resting place of very select company. Only The Evil Queen's elite are put to rest there.

Preachers. Prostitutes. Playwrights.

The Evil Queen is digging a new grave. She digs every new grave with her own cold hands. And she buries the dead herself.

The little girl died from the hideous effects of syphilis.

Only fourteen years old, delicate freckled hands tugging like mad at strawberry-colored hair, running barefoot, and screaming, screaming bloody-murder, all the while menstrual blood, tiny bits of black in the red, running down her soft naked legs. Small breasts, barely adult, nipples erect, they found her dead outside the butcher's shop.

Her once fair skin turned pale blue by the snow. And her baby fat was as hard as wood.

She will be buried next to Merlin.

"So many whores die from living life young. But few die too young."

Dirt is hitting the casket.

"Too many wives live not knowing they are dead. Long dead before they reach old age."

More dirt is hitting the casket.

On days when it seems like the rain will once again flood the earth, on days when the sky is one long angry cloud of continuous black, a hungry black monster eating every last bit of the innocent blue sky, only on those days, those days of horrid storm, barely any hint of light coming through, the sun denied, on those days, only on those days, The Evil Queen will pick you up, carry you like an infant, folded in her cold hard arms, and she will dance.

She will dance.

She will dance through her graveyard, she will sway through head-stones, spinning in circles, twirling, twirling, all the while the rain is coming down, coming down hard, pounding, pounding, pounding your infant flesh.

You can only see the sheets of water, sheets of angry water hitting your eyes, and The Evil Queen will rock you, rock you like a baby, rock you in her arms, in her cold cold arms, and she will dance, she will dance, and she will sing you lullabies.

The cemetery is built over the site of an ancient church. A church that was burnt to the ground, burnt to the ground by ancient whores. A church that most believe is best forgotten.

(Unholy Ground)

G O D ' S   A C R E

R O P E

THE EVIL QUEEN is sitting nude atop the window pane, her long legs dangle outside. She is enjoying the breeze against her skin. She gathers up all her pubic hair and casts it to the wind. A hideous black flag sails from her cunt.

You are thinking of how a man could climb that hair. Scale the tallest tower of the castle. A man could pull himself up, climb all-the-way-up to that cunt.

"My hair is so long I could hang a man. I could wrap it around the neck, wrap it around and around, and I could tie the end in a knot. I could let a man hang from this window, hang until dead. A noose made from pubic hair, no doubt a first in history."

Serpentine, the hair from her cunt is flapping, is snapping, akin to rope, or a whip, rising up, dropping down, sharp left, right, sliding like a snake, sliding back and forth, back and forth on the wind.

(flap, flap . . . snap, snap . . .)

N O O S E

L U P U S

THE EVIL QUEEN does not merely love men, she consumes men. Like the Big Bad Wolf, she gobbles men up. She eats men whole . . . every last bit . . . sometimes with one big bite . . . *gulp*.

You do not know if Poe died screaming while The Evil Queen loved him, while she gobbled him up. You imagine it took several bites, him being a genius.

Sometimes The Evil Queen goes running off into the woods, running stark naked, running like an animal, running on all fours.

When she returns, her hands and feet are dark from the forest dirt, and between her teeth she carries game.

A huntsman will hang dead from her mouth.

L Y C A N T H R O P Y

PSYCHO-SEXUAL SELF-EVALUATION

Questionnaire For The Reader
(Participation Is Not Optional)

PART 1: PROSE

1) Do you believe one word of this account? Yes (   ) No (   ) Decline to state (   )

2) Do you wish that The Evil Queen were more evil? Yes ( ) No ( ) Decline to state (   )

3) Have either The Evil Queen or the eunuch been developed adequately as characters in this work (i.e., do you feel that you understand, or do you feel that you "know," either one)? Yes (   ) No (   ) Decline to state (   )

4) Do you want there to be more explicit sex in the work? Yes (   ) No (   ) Decline to state (   )

5) Has the work, for you, so far carried any religious significance? Yes ( ) No ( ) Decline to state (   )

6) If yes, then what is it (25 words or less)?

_____

_____

_____

_____

_____

7) While reading this work, have you bothered to look up any word that was not in your vocabulary? Yes ( ) No ( ) Decline to state ( )

PART 2: POLITICS

1) Do you feel that the creation of new schools of sexual perversion is a viable undertaking for the artist of today? Yes ( ) No ( ) Decline to state ( )

2) If yes, then do you believe it is the quintessential undertaking? Yes ( ) No ( )

3) Do you believe that whores should be allowed to form guilds, unions, or other forms of legal assembly? Yes ( ) No ( ) Decline to state ( )

4) If art for art's sake has merit, then does sex for sex's sake (i.e., are they symbolically — if not socio-culturally — equivalent)? Yes ( ) No ( ) Decline to state ( )

5) Do you feel that The Church should adopt an official stance of repentance for the crimes it committed against witches during The Inquisition (i.e., mass, if not, serial murder), and that it should employ a program post haste that would commission it to fully apologize for those crimes? Yes ( ) No ( ) Decline to state ( )

6) During The Inquisition, how many witches were sentenced to death by The Church?   _____

7) What % of them were women?   _____

PART 3: PERSONALITY

1) In your opinion, should the human female have more than one clitoris? Yes ( ) No ( ) Decline to state ( )

2) If yes, then how many?   _____

3) If no, then please indicate your gender. Male ( ) Female ( )

4) Do you enjoy receiving anilingus? Yes ( ) No ( ) Decline to state ( )

5) Do you enjoy performing anilingus? Yes ( ) No ( ) Decline to state ( )

6) Is either Black or Red your favorite color? Yes ( ) No ( ) Decline to state ( )

7) How many sexual partners have you had? Over 50 ( ) Under 50 ( ) Decline to state ( )

EXTRA CREDIT

1) If you have ever solicited a whore, then check here. ( )

2) If you are (or ever were) a whore, then check here. ( )

BONUS QUESTIONS

1) Are you aware that all the varied religious and artistic schools of thought believe that prose, politics, and personality are ultimately identical? Yes ( ) No ( )

2) Are you aware that they are correct? Yes ( ) No ( )

Judging Performance On Psycho-Sexual Self-Evaluation

Part 1
1 Yes = 10 points	No = 5 points	Decline to state = -10 points
2 Yes = 10 points	No = 5 points	Decline to state = -10 points
3 Yes = 10 points	No = 5 points	Decline to state = -10 points
4 Yes = 10 points	No = 5 points	Decline to state = -10 points
5 Yes = 10 points	No = 5 points	Decline to state = -10 points
6 N/A		[see note below]
7 Yes = 10 points	No = 5 points	Decline to state = -10 points

Part 2
1 Yes = 10 points	No = 5 points	Decline to state = -10 points
2 Yes = 20 points	No = -20 points	
3 Yes = 10 points	No = 5 points	Decline to state = -10 points
4 Yes = 10 points	No = 5 points	Decline to state = -10 points
5 Yes = 10 points	No = 5 points	Decline to state = -10 points
6 20 points		-20 points [see note below]
7 20 points		-20 points [see note below]

Part 3
1 Yes = 10 points	No = 5 points	Decline to state = -10 points
2 10 points	5 points	-10 points [see note below]
3 -10 points		-20 points [see note below]
4 Yes = 10 points	No = 5 points	Decline to state = -10 points
5 Yes = 10 points	No = 5 points	Decline to state = -10 points
6 Yes = 10 points	No = 5 points	Decline to state = -10 points
7 Over 50 = 10 points	Under 50 = 5 points	Decline = -10 points

EXTRA CREDIT   BONUS QUESTIONS
1   20 points   1 Yes = 20 points No = -20 points
2   20 points   2 Yes = 20 points No = -20 points

[— Note, Part 1, Question 6: No points (it is only meant to help you gather your thoughts)]

[— Note, Part 2, Question 6: If answer is greater than or equal to 200,000 (two hundred thousand), then score is 20 points; if answer is less than 200,000 (two hundred thousand), then score is -20 points. — Note, Part 2, Question 7: If answer specifies that 90% or more the victims were women, then score is 20 points; if answer does not specify that 90% or more of the victims were women (i.e., your answer is less than 90%), then score is -20 points.]

[— Note, Part 3, Question 2: If answer is 15 or more, then score is 10 points; if answer ranges from 4 to 14, then score is 5 points; and if answer is less than 4, then score is -10 points. — Note, Part 3, Question 3: If Male, then -10 points; if Female, then -20 points]

Reading Scores On Psycho-Sexual Self-Evaluation

If you score *over* 245points, then you are perverted
If you score *under* 245points, then you are repressed

Record Test Score: _____

Record Test Date: _____

Signature of Tester: _____

[Final note concerning outcome of scores: This test is irrefutable]

PART TWO

Resurrection

[sound of hunting horn behind red curtain — curtain rises]

FRIGIDITY

YOU can ask yourself only one question, there is only one question to ask: has your experience with The Evil Queen, has your training, your molestation, has living with The Evil Queen made you a better, a superior, an altogether more authentic human being? — do you know yourself to be more?

You can answer yourself in only one way, there is only one answer to your question: yes — YES ! ! !

Footnote:

Maiden

Spinster

Vestal

Virgin

· vs.

Bawd

Courtesan

Cyprian

Delilah

Doxy

Drab

Fancy Woman

Fallen Woman

Harlot

Hooker

Leman

Meretrix

Mistress

Paphian

Prostitute

Quean

Slut

Streetwalker

Strumpet

Tart

Trollop

Trull

Whore

etc., etc., etc., . . .

P R O F L I G A C Y

SHULAMITE

Reaction to the cunt of The Evil Queen (Blake): With tears in his eyes he cries with joy: "Glory! Glory! Glory! — Excess! Excess! Excess!"

William is a shepherd, a shepherd walking through a field. He is walking slowly toward a young woman. The woman is standing before him. She is waiting, she is nude. Her arms hang loose at her sides. There is no tension in her naked body. She is calm, relaxed. Neither one of them are shy. Neither one of them feel shame. Both have their eyes wide open. Their eyes are double their normal size. A warm breeze gently teases her hair, tickles her between her legs.

When the shepherd reaches the woman, she helps him to undress.

William is running naked through the fields. Only his sandals are on. He is holding his penis, his penis is a gigantic blooming lily. The lily towers high above the fields, towers high above the shepherd. The young woman is giggling, she is running after William, tossing tiny pebbles at the giant lily. She kisses the pebbles before she tosses them. Both laugh and play as children do.

The shepherd finally collapses, falls onto his back. The woman falls upon him. They laugh, they smile. Both are breathing heavy. They rest beneath the shade provided by the lily.

Her eyes are doves. His eyes are nests. The doves take flight, fly high into the air, then swoop down, circle the young woman, circle the shepherd, then settle into the nests, the soft nests of William's eyes.

The woman stands, offers her hands to the shepherd. The shepherd accepts, her soft hands take his, she helps him rise. They walk without speaking, walk for a while, in silence, simply holding hands, simply being beautiful.

The woman's lips are ribbons of wet crimson. William loosens the fabric, takes hold of the ends, and skips away, like a child, pulling on the red, allowing more and more of it to be lifted by the wind, two streams of scarlet, like tails on a kite, swimming with, swimming through, the blue of the sky.

The longest kiss in history.

She lies on her back, spreads her legs, those soft young legs. The shepherd approaches, first on two legs, then on four, shepherd becomes stag, sandals become hooves, halo becomes antlers, and all the while, the woman is growing, her hair becomes grass, becomes trees, the arch of her back a mountain, her arms and legs become birds and beasts, her teeth become a flock of goats, her breasts become hills, her vulva a deep valley dividing the mountain, a stream follows the valley's course, clear water rushes over rocks, at the base of the mountain is an orchard of pomegranates, and flowers, such beautiful flowers, can be seen as far as the horizon.

With tears in his eyes he cries with joy: "Holy! Holy! Holy! — Excess! Excess! Excess!"

When William recovers from his vision, he runs home to write a poem.

BEATRICE

S P H I N X

Reaction to the cunt of The Evil Queen (Blake): With tears in his eyes he cries with grief: "Earthly! Earthly! Earthly! — Excess! Excess! Excess!"

William is a sage, a sage limping down a road. He leans heavy on his cane. The cobblestones hurt his feet. It is hot. He shades his eyes with his free hand. Looking forward, squinting against the sun, he sees that a woman is sitting on the rock fence that follows the road. He sees that she is nude. Her arms are folded. There is a universe of tension in her naked body. She is rigid, agitated. William does not notice. William feels too much shame to see past a nude woman to a woman who is nude. She is simply, she is evilly, nude. His eyes are half their normal size. They grow smaller and smaller with age. When he squints, his eyes disappear, his red face swallows them whole.

The sage attempts to walk past the woman, limping, one small eye on her nudity, one small eye on his shame, watching her, looking away, judging her, judging himself, acknowledging her only by ignoring her.

Simple . . . evil . . . nude . . .

She unfolds her arms.

She grabs his cane and begins to strike the sage about the eyes and groin.

William is rolling in agony atop the cobblestone road. There is dirt in his eyes, dirt mingled with bits of cane, bits of face. He is holding his penis, his penis is a tiny maggot. The woman is laughing, the woman is weeping, she is stabbing his eyes with his broken cane.

William's body lies like a rag in the gutter: wrinkled
                                                stained.

The Sphinx is examining the sage's body: sniff - circle - nudge - sniff. The Sphinx bends down, kisses the sage's forehead, begins cleaning his damaged eyes. William hears euphonic purring, feels a soft tongue licking his eyes.

                      (but the sage covers his eyes)

The Medusa is cradling the sage's body. The Medusa rocks the wounded sage in her arms. Serpent hair tickles baby. Each hair hisses lullabies for baby.

                      (but the sage covers his ears)

With tears in his eyes he cries with grief: "Worldly! Worldly! Worldly! — Excess! Excess! Excess!"

When William recovers from his vision, he runs home to write a poem.

MEDUSA

M A G A D

Reaction to the cunt of The Evil Queen (Nietzsche: Taken from the pages of his college notebook): "Wunderbar!!!"

Beautiful   Natural   Physical

Not once has she stepped foot in The City of God. No, her toes kiss the earth, not the sky. Indeed, she dances through The City of Man.

She glides and she shakes and she jumps and she flutters.
Free.

And the men adore her. Adore her dancing.

Barefoot   Pitter-Patter   Young Feet

She dances in the plaza: The Plaza of Man.
She dances in the garden: The Garden of Man.

On the roof-tops   In the alleys   Under the sheets

I shall not say she is heaven on earth. I would not presume to insult the earth.

But her eyes are like bright stars, bright stars to wish upon.
And she winks.

E R A D

FECULENCE

Reaction to the cunt of The Evil Queen (Nietzsche: Taken from the margin of a notebook, frantically written, while in the throws of a psychotic episode, induced by syphilis, near the end, near the bitter end, of his life): "Luba! Luba!! Luba!!! — Haz! Haz!! Haz!!! — Luba! Haz! Luba!! Haz!! Luba!!! Haz!!!"

kiss . . . dish of maggots . . . squirming . . . vile . . . maggot meat . . . and i lick her plate

touch . . . smear of excrement . . . hands . . . soiled . . . hanging dirt . . . and i suck her fingers

cunt . . . festering wound . . . toilet for vermin . . . chalice of filth . . . and i drink her pus

. . . why won't the dirty whore let me touch her?

PUTRESCENCE

POLYMORPHOUS PERVERSITY

OUR CUNT, WHO ART IN CUNT, HALLOWED BE THY CUNT. THY CUNT COME. THY CUNT BE DONE ON CUNT, AS IT IS IN CUNT. GIVE US THIS CUNT OUR DAILY CUNT. AND CUNT US OUR TRESPASSES, AS WE CUNT THEM THAT TRESPASS AGAINST US. AND CUNT US INTO TEMPTATION, AND DELIVER US NOT FROM CUNT. AMEN.

HETAERISM

VIDE INFRA

Lack of reaction to the cunt of The Evil Queen (Lilith) : "Oculus."

The Evil Queen is sitting on her throne, sitting naked, her legs could not be further apart.

"You have such beautiful eyes."

(O)   (O)

(O)   ___

<u>Footnote on the "wink"</u>:

> an "eye" for weakness
>
> cast an eager "eye"
>
> kept an "eye" on her servant
>
> caught her "eye"
>
> with an "eye" to the future
>
> the "eye" of the riddle
>
> a vulva, "my eye!" that's a cunt

V I D E   S U P R A

COUP DE GRACE

Additional reactions to the cunt of The Evil Queen: "Murder."

Two ghosts sit together at a ghostly table, drinking ghostly sangria, from ghostly goblets.

JUG THE FIRST

P: *Yes, it is much safer, much safer to love the dead. The dead are always dead. The dead forever remain ideal, remain perfect. No divorce, no betrayal, no "affairs." Especially if you barely knew your lover in life. Or, better yet, if you never knew your lover at all. Yes, much safer, and altogether more romantic.*

(pause)

Romance put aside, Christ is the best example.

M: *I should never have traded my secrets, kept all that knowledge to myself. I knew she knew things I didn't. But I assumed I knew more, thought I'd always be a step ahead, thought I'd win.*

(pause)

She deceived me.

JUG THE SECOND

P: *How dare she kill me! Rob me of my romantic life! The dead can never love the dead! God knows, one must be the lover, the other the beloved! One alive, one dead!*

(pause)

How dare she kill me!

M: *She killed me as well, but more important, she deceived me! The wisest man in Europe! Oh yes, she played it up! "Profusely thankful" for any scrap of lore I'd give her! "Profusely apologetic" for the meager quality of her trade! Always leading me to believe she had little left, and I, a world, a treasure trove, that I was Master!*

(pause)

She deceived me!

JUG THE THIRD

P: *Now I am alone, truly, utterly, totally, alone. Yes, I am dead. The ideal is irrelevant. I am dead.*

(pause)

Now I am dead.

M: *I should never have confronted her.*

(pause)

But she deceived me.

The ghostly jugs are empty.

Akin to motes being brushed by a feather duster, the ghosts slowly scatter, slowly disappear.

Q U I E T U S

LOOKING GLASS

THE EVIL QUEEN is admiring her cunt. She is squatting on the castle floor, beneath her cunt is a mirror, an antique hand mirror fashioned from silver.

The image of Pan is etched into the polished silver. In a happy jump, his hooves meet and *click* at his side. The god is smiling from ear to pointed ear.

"Do you wish to hold the mirror," The Evil Queen inquires, not once looking up from the reflection of her cunt.

"Your highness," you answer, in your perfected tone of mock distinction, your *butler's* voice, "nothing would give me greater pleasure."

SPECULUM

M O T H E R   T O N G U E

SYLLABLES
                    follicles

pubic hair
                                        proper nouns
        consonants
                    curls
                                        diphthongs
                        dandruff
                                            combing
braiding
                reading aloud
                                    hair style
                    accent
                        pig tails   widow's peak
correct spelling
                                    redhead   blonde
        brunet
                regional dialects
                                        tresses locks tuffs

                vocabulary
                        every sound an individual strand
every letter a hair to touch
                                familiar words

goatee

                                    Latin
            crew cut
                            Greek
                                        cut   curl   crop
fingers through the language
                                                soft

                        so soft
                                that hairy alphabet

Q U E E N ' S   E N G L I S H

PENITENCE

ECCLESIAL rings squeeze tight around pudgy fingers.

The poor fellow, the poor fat fellow. He always pretends he does not know the way, pretends he has never been to the dining room. And he waddles, in that red gown, like a gigantic tomato, a gigantic tomato with legs.

Once a year, one week before Lent, you show the bishop to the dining room.

(Waddle - Waddle - Waddle)

FASTING

PREDATOR

"SELF-REGARD is rooted in murder."

(The Evil Queen is talking in her sleep)

"When you murder, you establish yourself as murder-*er*, and your victim as murder-*ed*."

"One who is killer, one who is killed."
"One who eats, one who is eaten."

(The Evil Queen has been known to sleepwalk)

"I've heard the argument: MIGHT IS NOT RIGHT. And perhaps that is true, or at least, it should be true, at least within a closed human system. But let's be honest, people must eat, and if we cannot eat one another, then who?, then what?, is to be eaten? That's right, animals, plants and animals. And even if you only eat plants, those helpless, those defenseless, those delicious plants, don't fool yourself, you too are a murderer."

(The Evil Queen turns restless in her sleep)

"Vegetarians are consumed by a unique sense of guilt, a sense of guilt uniquely human, a sense of guilt for being human. Their shame is in knowing that to live is to kill. I understand the shame, but I do not respect it. If they truly wanted to break the cycle, at least their cycle, they would all go out into the vegetable gardens of the world, lie face down in the soil, allow themselves to starve, to die, to decompose, and allow the vegetables to consume them, for a change.

(The Evil Queen rises from her sleep to get a snack)

P R E Y

THE titles of books you wish you could check out of the public library:

ECCLESIASTICAL HISTORY OF THE ENGLISH CUNT

THE VARIETIES OF RELIGIOUS CUNT

THE EGYPTIAN BOOK OF THE CUNT

THE GOSPEL ACCORDING TO CUNT

THE RIME OF THE ANCIENT CUNT

THE BALLAD OF READING CUNT

A MIDSUMMER NIGHT'S CUNT

LETTERS TO A YOUNG CUNT

THE SCARLET CUNT

MEIN CUNT

AU REVOIR

YOU discover the following letter tucked under your pillow:

DEAREST DWARF,

You have been an exceptional pupil, to both me and The Evil Queen (she chose you well). As a student of evil, you are first-rate. I have enjoyed our witching hour liaisons, and I will miss them, truly. But, alas, you are nearing manhood — Telemachus too had to set out on his own. Your studies are over. I trust you will perform the ritual perfectly (indeed, perfection is required). You have memorized my instructions. Practice must yield to performance. Now it is up to you.

Good luck my darling Eunuch,

MEPHISTOPHELES

Less than one week to go. You neither dread nor look forward to it.

It simply must happen. It simply will happen.

AUF WIEDERSEHEN

BLACK MAGIC

NOW you are in a dream, a dream of anger and of violence, a dream of revenge. It is not your dream, that is, it is not solely your dream, but a collective dream, a dream for men, a male dream.

Friedrich Nietzsche, Edgar Allen Poe, William Blake, yourself, and Merlin, stand around the blazing pyre.

The Evil Queen is tied to the stake.

Merlin: "Black Magic!"

Blake: "Female Will!"

Nietzsche: "Bitch!"

You recall an incident from history, an incident concerning another witch: Joan of Arc. Joan was captured at Compiegn, tried for heresy by French clerics, clerics sympathetic to the English, and was burnt at the stake.

It is common knowledge that Joan's body was consumed entirely by the flames, that is, except for her heart. Her heart was found still beating atop the ash.

(unharmed)

You think of Joan as The Evil Queen catches fire, you think of Joan as The Evil Queen burns atop that huge pile of wood, you think of Joan when only the embers remain.

Wait, there it is, sitting atop the ash.
Wait, there it is!

"Look!" You tell your brothers. "Look!" And you point, you point to the ashes.

And there, there it is, that magnificent cunt, sitting atop the ash.

(unharmed)

Poe: "A nightmare after all."

FEMALE WILL

CHEF - D'OEUVRE

THE EVIL QUEEN as sculptress, poetess, architect:

Long white fingers explore black hair.

A large ruby ring swirls just above the tuft.

She positions her regal scepter, eases it in.

        Fingers moving faster.

        Ring a red blur.

        Scepter picks up speed.

        She bites her lower lip.

MAGNUM OPUS

CONSTANCY

"YES, I have had numerous servants over the years, more than I care to count, many a servant indeed. But you, my little dwarf, my faithful eunuch, are by far the best."

"Before you, not one lasted even a meager century, most expired without enduring even one decade of service. But not you, my tiny man, you are a true companion to evil."

"No matter what the chore, no matter what the duty, you accomplish it, without the slightest groan, and always with a smile. Yes, you have the most sincere smile I have ever seen. The most sincere smile on the most sincere face."

"Equanimity, equanimity lends honesty to evil."

"Equanimity, equanimity lends structure to evil."

"Equanimity, equanimity lends longevity to evil."

"You are equanimity incarnate, my little servant, without you, without your service, evil would lose all integrity."

FEALTY

DEJECTA

YOU are cleaning the privy. Scrubbing, scrubbing away the filth.

You are thinking of Martin Luther, of that Protestant revelation, of that great thought, that great notion, that revelation born of the privy.

You imagine Martin straining, straining his bowels, pushing, pushing out something long overdue.

He must have been constipated, that Protestant Father.

You imagine that revelation, being born, being born as he dropped the dirt.

How much of The Evil Queen, how much of her thought, are you scrubbing clean from the privy?

EXCRETA

M U S I C A L E

THE EVIL QUEEN owns a pipe organ, a very large pipe organ. In fact, it is larger than any pipe organ, from any church, in all the world.

An entire hall is set aside for the instrument.

Hundreds upon hundreds of pipes.

Guests often come to hear The Evil Queen play, play those miles of pipe. They dress in their best attire, pay huge sums to hear her music.

All agree that her playing is unique, that it is often brutal, and that it is always, always sad.

It is also agreed that she is a brilliant musician.

Profound melancholy resonates the hall.

What the audience does not know, what they can never know, is that the pipe organ does not so much play music, as torture souls. It is souls, not notes, that are released screaming from those miles of pipe.

And those souls, they never leave that music hall. They writhe about in pain, swim tortured, invisible, resonating, creating music, such sad music, bringing tears to the eyes of the audience.

And The Evil Queen plays, often with great emotion, quite dramatic, jerking movements, head up, head down, her fingers several slender blurs of white.

Thoroughly engrossed in the music.

And they swim, those souls, those tortured souls, sometimes for hours. But they always return, return to their home, return to that pipe organ.

The Evil Queen has gathered quite a following.

RECITAL

HAIR
BLACK LETTERS
WHITE PAGE SKIN

J U N T O

THE castle does have a ballroom, though it is seldom used. But it will be used tonight, it being Halloween.

The Evil Queen adores costumes: Vampires, Werewolves, Ghosts.

Of course many of her guests do not need costumes.

Banquet.

Black Mass.

Belly Dancers.

Succubi serve sangria.

No one throws a party like The Evil Queen.

C A B A L

E U C H A R I S T

CATHOLICS do not enjoy the topic, but the topic has been known to come up, that Catholics are cannibals.

The eating of a body, the drinking of blood, seems fairly straightforward, one would think.

True, they only eat one body, only one man is drained of blood.

Catholics do not enjoy the topic, but the topic has been known to come up, that Communion is as close to . . . Well, let's not embarrass the Catholics, especially the men.

F E L L A T I O

HERO

FIGURES you wished had shaped World History:

ALEXANDER THE CUNT
CHRISTOPHER CUNT
WILLIAM THE CUNT
ULYSSES S. CUNT
KARL VON CUNT
BILLY THE CUNT
SIGMUND CUNT
KUBLAI CUNT
EL CUNT

and
of course

JESUS CUNT

HEROINE

URSPRACHE

YOU admire her, admire her greatly.

Lilith was the first to utter the name of God.

For you, that utterance marks the beginning of history, when life began its slow dance with death.

She has told you the story, hundreds of times, how she spoke the unspeakable, and you love her, you love her a little more each time she tells it.

Only one thing could top that achievement, only one event. To speak, to utter, to articulate each and every word at once.

Imagine it, linguistic apocalypse, the end of history.

TETRAGRAMMATION

FELICITATION

THE WANDERING JEW comes skipping into the castle, skipping arm-in-arm with Lilith.

"Greetings, eunuch, I brought a friend."

Lilith is the only person who ever just *pops* in. It is customary to make an appointment. The Evil Queen is a busy Queen. But not Lilith. Whenever Lilith arrives, The Evil Queen drops everything, cancels all appointments, and the two will talk for hours.

The Wandering Jew comes skipping into the castle, skipping arm-in-arm with Lilith.

"Sorry to intrude, dwarf, but Lilith insisted that we just *pop* in."

You have seen The Wandering Jew before, maybe two hundred years ago. He was wandering England. The Evil Queen gave him food and lodging. He stayed no longer than a week.

You recall then that he was quite depressed, speaking little, anxious to continue wandering, but not possessing the wanderer's heart. Indeed, no wanderlust.

Yes, quite depressing.

But look at him now, skipping, arm-in-arm with Lilith, skipping like a child, and laughing, laughing loud happy laughs.

And here comes The Evil Queen, running down the staircase, running to meet her friend.

You watch her gather one arm from Lilith, one arm from The Wandering Jew. You watch as all three go skipping, go skipping out of the castle.

(skipping)

(arm-in-arm)

E U D A E M O N I S M

ARCHITECTURE

"EVIL QUEEN, may I speak with you?"

"Yes, you may speak."

"I have a question concerning this castle."

"What is your question?"

"Who built this castle, who designed it?"

(pause)

"I did, of course."

"This was once the site of an early Christian structure. Constructed, haphazard, mostly of wood."

"The men who lived here were the usual Christians, you know, real party poopers, always ranting on and on about sin, about Jesus, about hell."

"Well, back in those days, the Christians were few, though they believed they were the whole world."

"I led an attack, an attack on those party poopers."

"Over 2000 women, over 2000 whores, carrying torches, carrying sticks and stones."

"The fools should have ran, it was no surprise attack. We made quite the racket. You could hear us miles off."

"Their kneeling only made it easier for them to be killed."

(smile)

"I designed the castle myself, built it over the years from stones stolen from Christian roads, from Christian churches."

"That is one thing Christians are good for, stones."

"Building supplies."

ARCHITECT

CONVERSAZIONE

GUESTS who frequent the castle, guests adored by The Evil Queen:

THE GHOST OF CLEOPATRA VII
THE GHOST OF JOAN OF ARC
THE GHOST OF POPE JOAN
THE GHOST OF BOADICEA
THE GHOST OF DIOTIMA
THE GHOST OF SALOME
THE GHOST OF SAPPHO
THE WEIRD SISTERS
MORGAN LE FAY

and
of course

LILITH

SOIREE

PRINCE CHARMING

YES, it happens. It is rare, but it happens. A prince or a knight sneaks into the castle.

(uninvited guest)

You know, the usual. The brave lad is looking for a princess, a beauty. He always assumes he will find her sleeping.

If The Evil Queen is feeling extravagant, she will become a dragon, she will breathe fire.

If she is not feeling up to the dragon bit, she will simply invite the lad to supper, provide him with a hearty meal, become bored with his conversation, order the wine, and watch the lad slowly die of poison.

Hearty meal.

Sleeping beauty.

A lad is a lad.

(easy kill)

BRAVE KNIGHT

EXCERPTS RECOVERED FROM THE DIARY OF THE EVIL QUEEN

(Translated from The French)

Two Sisters, identical twins, both strawberry blonde, nude, their bodies adorned with delicate freckles, both very cute, are bound together, face-to-face, and I whip them, I whip them from freckled head to freckled toe, I whip them with their Father's belt. Then I ask my servant: "Do you not wish that you had a cock, so you could unload your spunk into the very faces of these beaten Sisters?"

I am in the confessional with the Priest. My right hand is holding a pistol to his head. My left hand is stroking his sweaty cock. I stroke him as he listens to confessions. After the last confessor leaves, I squeeze the trigger — *click.* His brains are thrown out like red garbage against the black wood. On my way home, I suck his spunk off my fingers.

The Alter Boy is lying on his back, trembling. His face is still a little red from my having slapped him around. Obedient, now, lying on his back, his mouth open, I stand over him, squat just above his face, and piss, piss into his trembling mouth.

I command my servant to be motionless. If he moves, then I will strike him. My servant is on his hands and knees, nude. He cannot even blink as he watches me suck my middle finger. I get behind him, push my wet finger up his ass. Then after, I place my dirty finger under his nose, command him to inhale, to inhale deeply, to take a big whiff.

The nun is begging me to free her, to allow her to go back to the nunnery. I agree to free her, if only she will grant me one wish. She agrees. The nun will lick my spittle from off the floor. I become aroused, so aroused, as I watch her lick my spit from off that dusty floor.

I have my servant watch as I direct the newlyweds. The groom is atop the bride, pulling her hair, biting her back, fucking her in the ass. I order my servant to tell the bride to beg for more, to beg her groom to fuck her, harder, fuck her harder in the ass. After he ejaculates, I command him to lick her, lick her clean, to eat his dirty spunk from out of her bleeding ass.

The soldier is placed within a narrow cage. He must kneel. After two weeks, his knees are broken. He is never fed. My servant and I stab him to death with red hot pokers.

I bend the Bishop over, loosen his clothes, reveal his buttocks. I beat him, beat his bare ass with his cane. He needs that cane to walk, to stand. He braces himself against a wall, his knees shaking. I order my servant to get a running start, to charge the Bishop at full speed. My servant runs, runs up at full speed, collides against the old man's legs, sends him, toppling, to the floor. As the Bishop writhes in pain, unable to rise, my servant and I take turns, take turns shitting, shitting atop the face, atop the face of that weeping old man.

The assassin was employed to poison the food of the local abbess. The poison causes the cunt to close, so as to never allow any menstrual blood to leave the body. The assassin reports that she died in great agony.

PART THREE

Ascension

and/or

Descension

[sound of dinner bell behind black curtain — red curtain drops]

G A R C O N

"I KNOW he takes you at night."

(you say nothing)

"I can smell his manhood on your breath."

(still, you say nothing)

"Do not worry, I shall not interfere."

(you take a step backward)

"I just wanted you to know, to know that I know."

(you take another step back)

"Please bring me my breakfast, my tomato juice and black pepper."

(pause)

"Bring me two glasses, I would love some company at breakfast, your company."

M A J O R D O M O

POTABLE

"DEAREST servant, I would like to drink, drink a lot. And I would love to drink with you."

"Care to be my drinking partner?"

She carries you, piggy-back, down into the wine cellar.

"Pick a barrel, dearest servant, pick any barrel at all."

So you walk back, walk back into the oldest section of the cellar, walk all-the-way-back.

"This one," you say, "this one on the end."

"Excellent choice!" She says, clapping her hands, jumping up and down like a little girl.

And the sound of her clapping is carried up the stairs.

(clap-clap-clap)

LIBATION

EPITHALAMIUM

A Virgin

I was barely thirteen
when your messenger came
bearing that lily.

He told how I
a dirty common girl
was to meet the king.

You knew I was promised
to that quiet man
but still you insisted.

Not even one kiss
or whisper to console
as you had your way.

And I
a virgin.

Footnote: Translated from Aramaic (circa. 1 B.C.)

NUPTIAL ODE

F R U I T

The Apple

What
did he expect
making me *so* red
saying I'm *so* bad
then leaving me
unattended?

Footnote: Translated from Proto-Malus (circa. 4004 B.C.)

F O R B I D D E N   F R U I T

GODHEAD

GODLY HEAD:

God's eyes that see you, are your eyes seeing God.

God's ears that hear you, are your ears hearing God.

God's nostrils that smell you, are your nostrils smelling God.

GODLY TORSO:

God's cock that ejaculates you, is your cock ejaculating God.

God's cunt that births you, is your cunt birthing God.

God's ass that shits you, is your ass shitting God.

GODHOOD

MULIEBRITY

IT WAS NOT UNTIL THE NINETEENTH CENTURY THAT AMERICAN WOMEN LAUNCHED A SOCIAL MOVEMENT WORTHY OF PUSHING HUMAN EVOLUTION FORWARD. INDEED, SHOULD NOT SUSAN B. ANTHONY, ELIZABETH C. STANTON, AND LUCRETIA C. MOTT REPLACE WASHINGTON, HAMILTON, AND JACKSON ON THE ONE, TEN, AND TWENTY DOLLAR BILL, RESPECTIVELY?

PS: BIG BEN, THE EMPIRE STATE BUILDING, AND THE EIFFEL TOWER SHOULD ALL BE REPLACED BY STATUES OF EMMA GOLDMAN.

PPS: IT SHOULD BE MADE LAW THAT THE LIKENESS OF JOSEPHINE K. HENRY APPEAR ON THE STATE FLAG OF KENTUCKY.

MONUMENT

COGITO, ERGO SUM

THE EVIL QUEEN has a philosopher in her torture chamber, a theologian. He is tied to The Rack. He is gagged. As she stretches him, she lectures him.

"Shite!"

"I *think,* therefore I am?"

"Shite!"

(S t r e t c H)

"We certainly *are* before we think!"

"What do you believe a newborn thinks? Shite! A newborn wants, a newborn needs, but a newborn does not think! But an infant surely is. Would you not agree?"

(S t r e t c H)

"How about, I *want*, therefore I am?"

"No, even better, I *need*, therefore I am?"

(S t r e t c H)

"What, too honest?"

"Not abstract?"

"Too pedestrian?"

"Not academic?"

"Am I leaving out Father Sky?"

"Shite!"

"Come back down to earth!"

(S T r e t C H)

"The body/mind dichotomy?"

"Shite!"

"Body *is* mind."

"Mind *is* body."

(S T r e t C H)

"Why is it that evil is always bodily, what you do, where you are? Why? Because evil is real! Evil is bodily!"

(S T r e t C H)

"I know, I know. Jesus taught that what you do in your mind is as sinful, *is as sinful*, as what you do, what you really do, with your body."

"Praise the Lord!"

"Jesus was right!"

(S T R e T C H)

"Mind and body, no dichotomy, only rhetoric, the rhetoric of shame, shame of the body."

(S T R e T C H)

"See evil."

"Hear evil."

"Speak evil."

(S T R e T C H)

"When was the last time you took advice from a monkey, a monkey wearing clothes?"

(S T R E T C H)

CARTESIANISM

AVARICE

SHE held the burglar by the neck, held him in the air, just above her head, squeezing his throat.

"So, you have not come for any sleeping beauty, but for treasure. At least you are grounded. You do not know how I loath romantics."

"But what to do with you?"

The Evil Queen scratched her head with one hand, thinking. Held the burglar up with her other hand, squeezing.

"I have it!" The Evil Queen said, dropping the burglar to the floor. "I have just the right idea!"

The long of the short of it was that the burglar would steal the crosses from off the tops of the local churches. It was understood that it would take some time, maybe a whole year. She was so delighted with the idea, the idea of possessing those crosses, that she would pay him, pay him gold, for every cross he stole for her.

She would get what she wanted, the crosses. He would get what he wanted, his life. And he would also get treasure, get gold.

The burglar was discovered stealing a cross from atop one of the local churches. He was chased down the street by some locals, caught, beaten, then hanged from a tree.

The Evil Queen did not get one cross. And the burglar did not get one piece of gold.

BURGLARY

CONNOTATION

The following words delight you

    1) *Volk*

    2) *Lebensraum*

The following word frightens you

    1) *Nazi*

DENOTATION

THE EVIL QUEEN: QUEEN OF EVIL !!!

e.g., WEREWOLF, WITCH

i.e., WHORE

BOYS

THE castle does get Peeping Toms. Now and then. Mostly children. Usually a group of boys.

You assume it takes one boy to bring up the idea, another to support it (to "second it"), and a third to actually lead the expedition. That would account for there usually being three, there usually being three boys.

Yes, sometimes there are more, maybe a few trailing behind the main three, but those boys are half ready to flee the scene. Those boys are halfway home before the main three realize they too should be running. Sometimes there are two, and there is the rare one, but those are always the older boys, and the castle gets very few of them.

Yes, it is mostly children, boys, in groups of three, who come to peep through the castle windows.

RASCALITIES

B E A U T Y   S L E E P

GIRLS are trained to take the role of princess.
Boys are trained to take the role of prince.

Good girls are to be found sleeping, to be awakened by the prince.
Brave boys are to be awake, so as to awaken the princess, customarily with a kiss.

So many vaginas, so many cunts, sleeping.
So many vaginas, so many cunts, eyes closed.

Remember girls, a girl cannot wink if a girl is sleeping.
A girl cannot wink if her eyes are closed.

S O P O R

DRAMATICS

THE three boys are chained together at the ankles.

(Peeping Tom chain gang)

First, The Evil Queen has the boys watch as she sharpens her knives, those long long knives.

(butcher knives)

Royal slipper on the peddle, blade sliding along stone wheel.

Grind, grind . . . sharpen, sharpen, sparks . . .

(very dramatic)

Second, The Evil Queen has the boys watch as she prepares the oven.

She asks the boys which wood they prefer, which wood for the fire. Do the boys prefer one scent of smoke to another?

(very theatrical)

The fire is roaring.

It is time to cook.

"Oh no," The Evil Queen exclaims, "only one can fit into the oven. I guess I must choose only one of you."

(holding her chin: thinking)

Snaps her fingers.

(SNAP)

"Wait, I have an even better idea. You boys will choose. You boys will choose who I will cook in this oven. Yes, you decide this matter between yourselves."

(the three boys *gulp* in unison)

"And no heroics, boys."

"No Three Musketeers."

"None."

T H E A T R I C S

S U P P E R

OR the two boys are dressed in their Sunday Best, even though it is Friday night.

"You boys look absolutely handsome," The Evil Queen says, rubbing both boys on the head, messing up their hair just a little.

You show the boys to the dining table, that world of wood, playground of carved dragons, carved serpents and griffins. A beautiful table.

You pull out their chairs.

The Evil Queen claps her slender hands.

(CLAP-CLAP)

"Bring our dinner, little helper, and make a plate for yourself."

You bring Bobby out on a platter, carry him high above your head, little Bobby Baptist, on a silver platter.

An apple in his mouth. He is cooked a golden brown. Sliced tomatoes decorate his corpse.

(silence while eating)

(everyone helps themselves to seconds)

(not one bit of Bobby is left)

"Bobby was our leader," the blonde boy says, breaking the silence.

"But Bobby was a bully," the redhead adds.

"He was two years older," the blonde continues, "two years older but half as bright."

"But we followed Bobby," the redhead says, more than a little happy that Bobby is gone, well, not really gone, but down in his tummy. "If we didn't follow him, he'd beat us up, rub our faces in dirt, stuff like that."

(BURP: blonde)

The redhead continues, "Bobby was sure good, can I have a little more sangria?"

LEADER

A N N A L S

EVENTS that you wish had shaped World History:

THE SPANISH-AMERICAN CUNT
THE FRANCO-PRUSSIAN CUNT
THE HUNDRED YEARS CUNT
THE AMERICAN CIVIL CUNT
THE PELOPONNESIAN CUNT
THE ENGLISH CIVIL CUNT
THE THIRTY YEARS CUNT
THE SEVEN YEARS CUNT
THE TROJAN CUNT

and
of course

THE PASSION OF CUNT

C H R O N I C L E S

THERE are, of course, two kinds of Death.

(compare)

NIGHT SOIL
&
BURIAL GROUND

(contrast)

NIGHT SOIL
vs.
BURIAL GROUND

S O M N A M B U L I S M

THE EVIL QUEEN IS SCREAMING IN HER SLEEP:

"MY DINING ROOM ! ! ! . . . MY BED CHAMBER ! ! ! . . . MY GRAVEYARD ! ! ! . . ."

MY DINNER GUESTS ! ! ! . . . MY SWEETHEARTS ! ! ! . . . MY DEAD ! ! ! . . ."

UNDER HER BREATH: ". . . LEBENSRAUM, LEBENSRAUM . . . VOLK, VOLK . . ."

N O C T A M B U L I S M

B E A U X   Y E U X

THE EVIL QUEEN IS SCREAMING WHILE AWAKE:

" MY LIPSTICK ! . . . MY EYE SHADOW ! ! ! . . .

**RED ! . . . BLACK ! . . . RED ! ! . . . BLACK ! ! . . . RED ! ! ! . . .
BLACK ! ! ! . . . RED ! ! ! ! ! ! ! ! ! . . ."**

UNDER HER BREATH: " . . . SCOWL . . . WINK . . . BITE . . . . KISS . . . ."

B E A U   I D E A L

B U L L Y

OR Bobby was dressed in his Sunday Best. And, indeed, it was Sunday.

"So, you are the fearless leader," The Evil Queen said, while brushing a few boyish black hairs from his eyes.

"That's right, I'm the bully. I'm the one who beats 'em up."

"And why do you beat them, my little bully," The Evil Queen asked, while pinching his boyish cheek, leaving a little red on the pink.

Boyish grin reached from ear-to-ear, and the imp said, "well, 'cause they needs a beatin', 'cause they needs ta feel."

The Evil Queen bent down, squatted, as if to urinate right there on the castle floor, squatted down to meet the bully eye-to-eye, and asked, "what do you mean, to feel?"

"Well, everybody else is tellin' 'em not ta feel. Mom, dad, priest, God," snickering, more than just a little, as he said God. "Yep, everybody but me is tellin' 'em, orderin' 'em, not ta feel."

The Evil Queen stared deep into the bully's big brown eyes.

"I tell 'em don't listen ta yur parents, don't listen ta yur priest. But they never listen ta me," he said, puffing himself up, folding his arms. "So, after they come home from church, after they come home from *Con-Fes-Sion*," exaggerating each syllable, in his best brat tone, "I beats 'em, I beats 'em up good."

The Evil Queen just squatted there, smiling, her wide dragon smile.

"I bully 'em inta lyin', lyin' ta their parents, lyin' ta their priest. Why tell those grown-ups the truth, they only lie ta us kids," Bobby said, now holding hands with The Evil Queen, now walking side-by-side to the kitchen.

"Bobby, you can have anything you want for breakfast, anything. Pick your favorite. There are no grown-ups here."

"You don't know how many times I had ta beats 'em up before they'd follow me to this spooky castle," he said, while eating with his mouth open, while bits of ice cream flew out of his mouth.

TOUGH LOVE

DIPLASIOCOEIA

THE EVIL QUEEN has turned another prince into a frog.

(ribbit - ribbit)

"You know the drill. I know you have read the script."

"If the princess kisses you, you will return to your princely form."

"Just think: no more webbed feet
no more green skin
no more tasty flies."

"Of course, I am not quite sure how the princess will find you, let alone kiss you, her being asleep and all."

"And as we both know, the princess is a deep sleeper."

"Perhaps you can place a pea under her mattress?"

(ribbit - ribbit)

(ribbit - ribbit)

OSCULATION

FUNDAMENT

GREY eye squinting in the midst of heart-shaped white.

Puckered starfish.

Asshole.

Satanic rapping on that most forbidden door to The City of Man.

Forbidden kiss.

Anilingus.

Licking ass is a declaration of independence.

Licking ass is revolutionary.

Never transcendental.

Always terrestrial.

                          (slurp, slurp . . . slurp, slurp, suck)

The Evil Queen on her evil hands and knees.

You behind her, licking her evil anus.

Evil throat gulping, gulping sangria.

(slurp, slurp . . . slurp, slurp, suck)

The Evil Queen raises her viper-slim arm, raises her chalice of sangria, up up, high high to heaven, and says:

To the misogyny of Nietzsche
and the lunacy of Blake.

(suck, suck . . . suck, suck, slurp)

FUNDAMENTAL

S U C K L I N G

THE EVIL QUEEN, bitch, nursemaid of monsters.

Each and every clitoris, nefarious tit, each a pap for creatures, for creatures of the night.

How you miss that puppy, your role as baby beast.

Infant evil, nursing on thorns — spit, piss, or shit, infants know their milk.

N O U R I S H M E N T

CEREMONIAL

YOU remember the last night you were buggered by The Devil, the last night The Devil fucked you up the ass.

(Graduation Night)

You were always a little surprised, a little surprised he could push his whole cock up your ass, up your tiny dwarfen ass.

(Every Evil Inch)

But, like The Devil always said:

> *With patience and a stick of butter*
> *a man can accomplish anything.*

You loved the feel of pubic hair against your bottom, the feel of testicles bouncing lightly against you . . . forked tongue licking sweat off the back of your neck, horns grinding against your shoulder blades . . . all the while pretending, pretending that you, that you were The Evil Queen.

(Reverie)

His lessons had ended the night before, this buggery was simply ritual, a rite of passage, a butt-fucking-farewell.

You remember that he left you with this advice:

A man's cunt is his asshole.

It was a bonus that he ejaculated while still deep inside you. You adored him leaving it inside you, leaving that bit of himself behind.

And at breakfast the following morning, The Evil Queen asked if you had slept well. And, feeling Satan oozing from you, feeling Satan leaking, dripping, creeping from you, creeping from your ass, you answered with a smile:

"I never slept better in all my life."

A D I E U

V E R A C I T Y

THE EVIL QUEEN bats her long lashes, closes her left eye, *WINKS*, then, akin to some overpaid actress, pushes her lips into the shape of a heart.

(S M A C K)

. . . mark of red lipstick atop the monk's bald head.

SCENARIO

The Neo-Platonist — i.e., "The Monk" — is hanging nude from the ceiling of the torture chamber. Chains suspend him: hands directed toward Heaven, feet directed toward Hell. Folds of skin hang from the sides of the metal cuffs. Blood runs down his arms, blood drips from his ankles. A table is placed in front of The Monk. The table comes up to his torso. A thumbscrew is attached to the table. The Monk's penis is in the thumbscrew.

"The cosmos is a cunt."

(T W I S T)

"An ever lasting, never ending, cunt."

(T W I S T)

"A hairy chalice, a fishy grail, which has its center everywhere and its circumference nowhere."

(T W I S T)

"A vaginal mobius strip, with all of us, with each and everything, making up the totality of the cosmic cunt."

(T W I S T)

"The venereal micro and macro being the only constant truth."

(T W I S T)

"Truth, Monk? Cunt is Truth!"

(P U L P)

SILENCE, THEN

THE SCREAMS OF THE MONK ECHO THROUGH THE
TORTURE CHAMBER

FADE TO BLACK

V E R I D I C A L I T Y

ANATHEMATIZATION OF THE CUNT
IS NEVER AN ADEQUATE RESPONSE
TO THE CUNT

A R S E N A L

INVENTIONS that you wished had shaped World History:

KENTUCKY LONG CUNT
SUBMACHINE CUNT
RECOILLESS CUNT
MUSTARD CUNT
GATLING CUNT
12-GAGE CUNT
B-52 CUNT
H-CUNT
A-CUNT

and
just imagine it

ARMOR PIERCING CUNT

A R M A M E N T

MATURATION

THE EVIL QUEEN is lying atop her bed, nude. Her pale arms are stretched out like Christ. Her bed is made.

Her eyes are closed, but you know she is awake. She has had insomnia for close to a century.

You place the black doctor's bag atop her cunt, open it length-wise, open it like the lips of a gigantic cunt . . . *CRACK*.

You place the instruments on her white belly: scissors, hatchet, ice pick, pliers.

(wide wide smile — wide smile of proud mother)

A thunderstorm rages outside the castle.

She does not resist as you bind her hands and feet to the four-poster bed.

Red rope for the hands.

Black rope for the feet.

First, you break her fingers, break one finger at a time.

You snap those slender fingers with your pliers . . . *SNAP.*

You do the same to her toes.

Now you pull out her teeth, one-by-one, yanking hard on the pliers.

After sucking each clean of blood, you swallow those white bones . . . *GULP* . . . *GULP* . . . *GULP* . . .

Next, employing the ice pick, you take out her eyes.

Dangling those two orbs from their strings of gore, dangling them over your head, you suck them, one after the other, suck them down, suck them whole, without ever biting, feeling them *S L I D E* down your throat.

You suck them down whole and slurp those strings of gore like spaghetti.

Starting from the top, you slowly move down, snipping off each clitoris with your scissors . . . *SNIP* . . . *SNIP* . . .

After placing those bits of pink meat into the chalice, the chalice
containing your penis, you go back to her open wounds, and nurse,
nurse like a hungry puppy, a hungry puppy to its bitch.

You untie her, command her to roll onto her stomach, rebind her,
begin the procedure over again, top to bottom
                                      . . . *SNIP* . . . *SNIP* . . .

Then you have her crawl on her hands and knees, crawl down the
stone staircase, crawl down into the dungeon, all the while kicking,
kicking at her broken fingers, her broken toes.

You lead her like a bitch, noose around her neck, black-rope-leash.

You submit her to rope torture, binding her white limbs to red rope, raising her high into the air, then letting her . . . *D R O P* .

The red ropes break her fall, break her fall about a foot before hitting the dungeon floor.

You repeat this, over and over: RISE-DROP-RISE-DROP-RISE. You repeat this until you break every connection, dislocate every one of her joints.

Then you whip her, whip her violently with black rope.

(the sound of a baby crying between each crack of the whip)

While she is suspended, you pelt her with tomatoes.

You enjoy watching them break, in red explosions, as they collide against her broken physique. You especially love the ones that break against her face.

It is so beautiful, how the red of the tomato merges with the red of her wounds, how the fruit mingles with the blood, the marriage of red, *R E D - O N - R E D*.

And as she is still suspended, you employ the ice pick, gouge out her sex, cram that huge cunt into your mouth, slurping up every hair.

Then you venture out into the thunderstorm, go out into the rain.

You scale the tallest tower, reach the top, puke up the cunt. You place the cunt on top of the lighting rod, pierce it through the metal, then climb back down.

Admiring the thunder, you await the fortuitous strike.

You howl with the storm as that cunt catches fire!

You go back to the dungeon, lower her to the floor, begin hacking, hacking away at her body with the hatchet
                                        . . . HACK . . . HACK . . .

You hatchet away, with heavy blows, dismembering white meat, white meat framed in red.

When complete, you hang those hunks of meat from meat hooks, allowing the blood to drain . . . D R I P - B Y - D R I P . . . into empty wine barrels.

You take her ass and severed head back to her bed chamber. You take her hands and feet outside.

The castle has a black goat, a goat much loved by The Evil Queen. You take her feet to that black goat, watch as it devours the pale meat, those dead feet.

You think it fitting, allowing the goat to eat her feet. She loved that goat, loved to kick it about. It brought her such joy, kicking that goat.

Then you nail her dead hands to a dead tree behind the castle.

And though it is storming, crows appear, like black rain, black crows descend to devour those white hands.

Lifting her ass from the bed, you take it to the kitchen.

First you prepare the oven, then you prepare the ass.

You cut the white ass up into fine cubes, cut up plenty of tomatoes, make a stew, a tomato-buttocks-stew.

Cooking, you stir, adding sugar, some salt and pepper, various spices, various herbs.

When the stew is ready, you eat every bit, every last drop, you even lick the bowl.

Still hungry, you go to the chalice.

You bring the chalice to the pantry, take down the jar of sugar, begin spooning heaps of sugar into the wine.

While you stir, you watch the white dissolve into the red.

You raise the chalice to your lips, begin drinking deeply, gulping down that thick red. You feel each clitoris pass between your lips, slide down with the sanguineous syrup, and you feel your soggy cock, following that sweet red, follow that sweet red down your gulping throat.

Satisfied, you decide it is time to relax.

You take the blood gathered in the wine barrels to the bath chamber, fill that grand tub with the blood of The Evil Queen.

You take a long bath.

As you relax, you read from her journals of automatic writings.

After reading each entry, you tear the page out, place it over the flame of your reading candle, and watch as it burns, turns to ash, ash falling into your bath, falling into the blood of The Evil Queen.

(you cry yourself to sleep)

You sleep the entire next day.

When you awake the following morning, you are no longer a dwarf.

You are a giant.

You are eight feet tall.

And you are no longer a eunuch.

You possess a gigantic cock.

You go outside into the calm morning, note the pleasant breeze, then climb back up that tower to get the cunt.

Damaged from the lightening, soaked through-and-through from the storm, you regard its beauty, the cunt that fucked the storm.

Erect, you position the cunt, push the mangled meat down, smearing wet gore as you pierce the cunt with your cock.

You descend, go back into the castle, take the cunt into the privy, ring it like a wet cloth over the hole, dropping soiled water onto dirt.

Next, you go to the library, take a book from off the shelf, read aloud to the cunt:

Slang and its Analogues.

(cunt breaks water as you read the last page)

You close the book, set it down, then devour every last bit of that wounded cunt.

Licking your lips, you walk to her bed chamber.

You hold the severed head, combing her hair, kissing her where she once had eyes, where she once had teeth. You feel that wonderful strangeness. You love the feeling. Looking down at the sensation, you see that your cock is huge, is again erect.

First you fuck the softness of her toothless mouth.

Next, you fuck the gore of her eye sockets.

Last, you turn her severed head over, fuck her throat, fuck her right up the esophagus, until you unload your spunk.

You spend the rest of the day moving everything flammable. Everything that can burn you move into the library.

Walking away, you leave the castle behind, ignoring the towers of billowing smoke.

In one hand, you hold a jug of sangria.

In your other hand, you hold your cock.

Nude, you walk, gulping sangria, stroking your gigantic cock.

(*GULP...GULP...*)

(*STROKE...STROKE...*)

SUPPLANTATION

A P O C A L Y P S E (a n d /

FACT: THE VICTORY OF THE EVIL QUEEN'S CUNT
IS BOTH INEVITABLE AND EMINENT

PURPOSE: RADICAL DEVIRGINIZATION OF THE EVIL QUEEN,
OF THE UNIVERSE, OF THE WORLD, OF EACH AND EVERY
HUMAN BEING (WHETHER ALIVE OR DEAD)

FUTURE PARADIGM: APOTHEOSIS AND/OR ABOMINATION
(WINK) OF THE EVIL QUEEN

PRESENT STATE OF EVIL : FOR THE MAJORITY OF HUMANITY
THE EVIL QUEEN DROPS INTO THE PRIVIES OF THE WORLD,
BUT THE NUMBERS ARE GROWING FOR THOSE WHO
EM-BRACE HER AS FERTILIZER, AS SOBERING
NIGHT SOIL

BEHOLD: THE EVIL KING DEPARTS, CARRYING A JUG,
CARRYING THE PRINCIPLE OF EVIL
INTO THE MODERN ERA

SANGRIA ! ! ! ! ! ! ! ! !

o r) M E T A M O R P H O S I S

NOTES:

THE
bEginNingD

PSYCHO-SEXUAL
GLOSSARY
WORDS INDISPENSABLE for
THE EXEGESIS of OCCIDENTAL PERVERSION

[Nefarious Lexicon]

ADIEU noun [a (fr. L ad = to, near) + Dieu (fr. L Deus = God)] : FAREWELL

AMBROSIA noun [ambrotos (immortal), akin to brotos (mortal) — more at MURDER] : food of the gods

AMOUR noun [amare (to love)] : an illicit love affair

AMOUR PROPRE : FRENCH = LOVE OF ONESELF (self-esteem)

ANILINGUS (also ANILINCTUS) noun [anus + lingus or linctus (act of licking)] : erotic enjoyment achieved by oral stimulation of the anus — i.e., to lick ass (compare CUNNILINGUS, CUNNILINCTUS)

ANNALS noun [L annales, fr. pl. of annalis (yearly)] : historical records (see CHRONICLES)

ANNULMENT noun [ne (not) + ullus (any) + men (men : suffix denoting concrete result] : pronouncement declaring a marriage invalid

ANTEDILUVIAN noun [ante (before, in front of) + diluvium (flood)] : of or pertaining to the time before the biblical DELUGE

ANTHROPOPHAGUS noun [anthrop (man) + phagos (eating)] : MAN-EATER (cannibal)

APOCALYPSE noun [Gk apokalypsis, fr. apokalyptein (to uncover)] 1 : REVELATION   2 : ARMAGEDDON

APOSTASY noun [apostasia (revolt)] : renunciation of a religious faith

APOTHEGM noun [apophthengesthai (to speak out)] : short, pithy, and instructive saying (see APHORISM)

APOTHEOSIS noun [apotheoun (to deify)] 1 : DEIFICATION   2 : QUINTESSENCE

ARCHITECT noun [architekton (master builder), fr. archi (chief) + tekton (builder)]: one who designs buildings

ARCHITECTURE noun 1 : the art or science of building   2 : a unifying or coherent form or structure

ARMAMENT noun 1 : a military force   2 : arms and supplies (for war)

ARSENAL noun : a collection of weapons

ASSHOLE noun : ANUS (i.e., the posterior opening of the alimentary canal — i.e., an erotogenic zone)

ATHENAEUM noun [Athenaeum, a school in ancient Rome for the study of arts, fr. Gk Athenaion, a temple of Athena] : a room in which books are kept for use

AUF WIEDERSEHEN [till seeing again] : GERMAN = FAREWELL

AU REVOIR [till seeing again] : FRENCH = GOOD-BYE

AUT CAESAR AUT NIHIL : LATIN = EITHER A CAESAR OR NOTHING

AUT CAESAR AUT NULLUS : LATIN = EITHER A CAESAR OR A NOBODY

AUTOMATIC WRITING noun : writing without conscious purpose, as if possessed, or inspired, and often lacking awareness (trance?) as the act is being performed

AVARICE noun [L avaritia, fr. avarus (avaricious), fr. avere (to covet)] : GREEDINESS, CUPIDITY

AZRAEL noun : DEATH

BEATRICE : Dante's Spiritual Lover (see Paradiso)

BEAU IDEAL : FRENCH = IDEAL BEAUTY (the perfect type or model)

BEAUTY SLEEP noun (see PRINCE CHARMING)

BEAUX YEUX : FRENCH = BEAUIFUL EYES (beauty of face)

BIBLIOLATER noun [biblio (book) + later (worshiper)] 1a general : one who is overly devoted to books   b specific : one who is overly devoted to The Book — i.e., The Bible   2a general : obsession with and usually (unconscious) erotic interest in books   b specific : sexual perversion in which The Bible is the preferred sexual object

BIBLIOTHECA noun [biblio (book) + theke (case)] : a collection of books

BIBULOUSNESS noun [bibere (to drink)] 1 : the state of being fond of alcohol (often excessive fondness)   2 : the act of consuming alcohol (often consuming to excess)

BILLET-DOUX noun [billet doux (sweet letter)] : FRENCH = LOVE LETTER

BLACK MAGIC noun : magic employed for evil purposes

BOYS noun : male children (from birth to puberty)

BRAVE KNIGHT noun : an often young, and always romantic, fool

BRUNETTE noun : someone who has dark hair (e.g., black)

BULLY noun [modif. of D boel (lover), fr. MHG buole] 1 archaic : SWEETHEART   2 contemporary : someone habitually cruel to others weaker than him or herself

BURGLARY noun : the act of breaking and entering (usually at night) with the intent to commit a crime (especially thief)

CABAL noun [F cabbale (cabala, intrigue, cabal) fr. ML cabbala (cabala), fr. LHeb qabbalah (received [lore])] : a number of persons (or a number of groups) secretly joined to bring about usurpation (especially political usurpation)

CAPUT noun : LATIN = HEAD

CAPUT CORVI : LATIN = HEAD OF THE RAVEN (term used in alchemical manusripts)

CARTESIANISM noun [NL cartesianus, fr. Cartesius Descartes] : of or relating to Rene Descartes or his philosophy

CEREMONIAL noun : a ceremonial act, action, or system

CHEF-D'OEUVRE [leading work] : FRENCH = A MASTERPIECE

CHRONICLES noun : continuos and detailed historical accounts of events arranged in order of time

CLITORIDES noun [plural form of clitoris] : small erotogenic organs homologous to the penis(es) of the male

COGITO, ERGO SUM : NEW LATIN = I THINK, THEREFORE I AM (principle stated by Rene Descartes)

CONNOTATION noun : something suggested by a word or thing — i.e., IMPLICATION (compare DENOTATION)

CONSTANCY noun 1a : FORTITUDE   b : FIDELITY, LOYALTY

CONVERSAZIONE noun [It conversation] : a meeting for conversation (especially about art, literature, or science)

CORNUA noun [plural form of cornu] : horn-shaped anatomical structures

CORPUS DELICTI : LATIN = BODY OF THE CRIME

CORVUS : LATIN = RAVEN

COUP DE GRACE : FRENCH = STROKE OF MERCY (e.g., death blow, decisive act)

CRUCIFER noun [crux (cross) + fer (bearing)] 1 general : someone who carries a cross   2 specific : someone who carries a cross at the head of an ecclesiastical process

CUNT noun [ME cunte; akin to MLG kunte (female pudenda), MHG kotzo (prostitute); akin to OE cot (den)] : FEMALE PUDENDA

DAILY MISSAL noun [missa (mass)] : a book containing all that is to be said and done at mass for an entire year (e.g., the Liturgical Calendar, the Holidays of Obligation, the Vespers for Sunday, etc. — i.e., a cleric's manual)

DECOLLATION verb transitive [de (away) + collum (neck)] : BEHEAD

DEICIDE noun [deus (god) + cida (to kill)] 1 : the act of killing a god (or killing God) 2 : the killer of a god (or God)

DEIFY noun [deus (god) + ficare (make)] : to make a god of (to make God)

DEJECTA noun : FECES, EXCREMENT

DEMONOLOGY noun [daemon (evil spirit) + logia (doctrine : theory : science)] : the study of demons

DENOTATION noun : a direct or specific meaning as distinct from an implied or associated idea (compare CONNOTATION)

DER GEIST DER STETS VERNEINT : GERMAN = THE SPIRIT THAT EVER DENIES (applied originally to Mephistopheles)

DILUVIUM : LATIN = DELUGE (flood)

DIPLASIOCOEIA noun : FROG(S)

DIRGE noun [ME dirige (i.e., the Office of the Dead), fr. the first word of a LL antiphon, fr. L imper. of dirigere (to direct)] : a song or hymn expressing grief or lamentation (especially used in conjunction with funeral or memorial rites)

DOCUMENT noun [documentum (official paper)] 1a : official or original paper relied on as the basis, proof, or support of something b : something that serves as evidence or proof

DRAMATICS noun : dramatic behavior or expression

ELEGY noun [elegos (song of mourning)] : a song or poem expressing grief or lamentation (especially for the dead)

EMETOPHILIA noun [emetikos (causing vomiting), fr. emein (to vomit) + philia (friendship), fr. philos (dear)] : sexual excitement derived from vomiting and/or being vomited on (aka., "Roman Shower")

EPISTLE noun [epistola (letter)] 1 general : LETTER (especially a formal or elegant letter)   2 specific : one of the letters approved as a book for The New Testament

EPITHALAMIUM noun [L & Gk; L epithalamium, fr. Gk epithalamiom, fr. epi (on, at, beside) + thalamos (room, bridal chamber)] : a song or poem in honor of a bride and groom

ERAD : OLD HIGH GERMAN = EARTH (barbarian vernacular)

EUCHARIST noun [eucharistos (grateful)] : Christian sacrament in which bread and wine are partaken of as a commemoration of the death of Christ (note : see Gospel of John chapter 6; see TRANSUBSTANTIATION)

EUDAEMONISM noun [eudaimonia (happiness), fr. eudaimon (having a good attendant spirit, happy), fr. eu (good) + daimon (spirit)] : a theory that the highest ethical goal is happiness and personal well-being

EUNUCHISM noun : the practice of depriving a man or boy of his testes or external genitals (note : often a prerequisite for a male employed as a palace chamberlain or a male placed in charge of a harem)

EUPHEMISM noun [euphemos (auspicious) + pheme (speech)] : an agreeable or inoffensive expression used in place of one that may offend or suggest something unpleasant

EXECRATION noun [L exsecratus, pp. of exsecrari (to put under a curse), fr. ex + sacr (sacer = sacred)] : the act of cursing or denouncing (or the curse or the denouncement so uttered)

EXCRETA noun : EXCRETIONS

EXEGESIS noun [exegeisthai (to explain, interpret)] : an explanation and/or critical interpretation of a text or texts

EXTREME UNCTION noun : a sacrament in which a cleric anoints someone who is critically ill or injured and prays for that person's recovery and salvation

FAIT ACCOMPLI : FRENCH = ACCOMPLISHED FACT (i.e., a thing accomplished and presumably irreversible)

FASTING noun : the act or practice of abstaining from food

FEALTY noun 1 : the fidelity of a vassal to his lord   2 : intence fidelity

FECULENCE noun : FECES

FELICITATION noun : to be happy or fortunate

FELLATIO noun [fellare (to suck)] : oral stimulation of the penis — i.e., to suck cock

FEMALE WILL noun [Blakean Term] : read Blake's Jerusalem, The Mental Traveller, etc.

FERULE noun : an implement (usually a flat piece of wood — e.g., paddle, ruler) employed for the spanking of a child

FIDUS ACHATES noun : LATIN = FAITHFUL ACHATES (trusty friend)

FORBIDDEN FRUIT noun [fr. "the forbidden fruit" of the Garden of Eden in Gen 3: 2-19] : an immoral or illegal pleasure

FRANCOPHILE noun : someone who has a great interest in the nation of France, French culture, (and especially) the French language (i.e., someone who has a great love of anything French)

FRIGIDITY noun [frigus (frost, cold)] : marked or abnormal indifference to sex (especially in woman)

FRUIT noun [L fructus (fruit, use), fr. fructus, pp. of frui (to enjoy, have the use of)] : see FORBIDDEN FRUIT

FUCK noun or verb [of Gmc origin, prob. fr. or akin to D fokken (to breed — i.e., cattle), fr. MD, push, thrust, copulate; akin to Sw dial. fock (penis)] : COPULATION, COPULATE

FUNDAMENT noun 1a : BUTTOCKS b : ANUS

FUNDAMENTAL noun 1a : PRIMARY b : BASIC

GARCON noun [F, boy, servant, fr. OF, prob. of Gmc origin; akin to

OHG recchio (banished man)] : WAITER

GERMANOPHILE noun : someone who has a great interest in the nation of Germany, German culture, (and especially) the German language (i.e., someone who has a great love of anything German)

GODHEAD noun [ME godhed, fr. god + hed (hood)] 1 : divine nature or essence (i.e., DIVINITY)   2 : the supreme or ultimate reality (i.e., GOD)

GODHOOD noun [ME godhod, fr. OE godhad, fr. god + had (hood)] : divine nature or essence (i.e., DIVINITY)

GOD'S ACRE noun : CHURCHYARD (burial ground)

GONOCENTRIC adjective [gonos (procreation, seed) + kentron (center)] (ca. 1910) 1a general : having sex as a central interest   b specific : having one's own sexual drive as a central interest   2: characterized by or based on the atti-tude that sex is the central motive of behavior (e.g., Darwinism, Freudianism) —- see GONOCENTRISM noun

HARUSPEX noun [haru (akin to chorde gut) + spex (fr. specere to look)] : diviner in ancient Rome who based predictions on the entrails of sacrificial animals

HAUTEUR noun [haut (high)] : ARROGANCE (see HAUGHTINESS)

HAZ : OLD HIGH GERMAN = HATE (barbarian vernacular)

HERO noun : male equivalent of HEROINE

HEROINE noun : mythological or legendary figure often of divine descent endowed with great strength or ability

HETAERISM noun : in J. J. Bachofen's theory of history, that initial state of "primitive promiscuity" from which matriarchy later arose

HETERODOXY noun [heter (other : different) + doxa (opinion)] : UNORTHODOX (unconventional)

HIERODULE noun [hieros (sacred : holy) + doulos (slave)] : a slave employed in the service of a temple

HOMUNCULUS noun : a little man (e.g., dwarf)

INHUMATION noun [in (into) + humus (earth)] : the act or process of burying

INAMORATA noun : a woman whom one has falling in love and/or has intimate relations with

INTEGUMENT noun [in (to) + tegere (cover)] : something that covers or encloses (e.g., skin, membrane)

INTERNECINE adj [inter (among) + necare (to kill)] : mutually destructive

JUNTO noun [Sp junto (to join)] : a group of persons joined for a common purpose

KHARYBDIS noun : female sea monster in Homer's Odyssey notorious for pulling men down to their deaths (note : paired with Skylla, Kharybdis has been interpreted as representing the ultimate in feminine repulsion)

LANGUE noun [lingua (language)] : a linguistic system (compare PAROLE)

LEADER noun : a person who has commanding authority or influence

LIBATION noun [L libation, libatio, fr. libatus, pp. libare (to pour as an offering); akin to Gk leibein (to pour)]   1 : an act of pouring (a usually alcoholic) liquid as a sacrifice (e.g., to a god)   2 : the act or instance of ceremonial drinking   3 : BEVERAGE (especially alcoholic)

LOGION noun [logos (word)]   1 general : a saying   2 specific : a saying attributed to Jesus Christ

LOOKING GLASS : MIRROR

LUBA : OLD HIGH GERMAN = LOVE (barbarian vernacular)

LUPUS : LATIN = WOLF

LYCANTHROPY noun [lykos (wolf) + anthropos (man)] : the assumption of the form of a wolf (see WEREWOLF)

MAGAD : OLD HIGH GERMAN = MAIDEN (barbarian vernacular)

MAGNUM OPUS [great work] : LATIN = MASTERPIECE

MAJORDOMO noun [Sp mayordomo or obs. It maiordomo, fr. ML major domus (chief of the house)] : BUTLER, STEWARD

MALEDICTION noun [male (badly) + dicere (to speak, say)] : CURSE

MALEFACTION noun : an evil deed (CRIME)

MARIOLATRY noun : excessive veneration of The Virgin Mary (worship?)

MASOCH, VON [Leopold von Sacher-Masoch (died 1895)] : German novelist (see MASOCHISM)

MATURATION noun [fr. L maturus (ripe); akin to L mane (in the morning), manus (good)] : the process of becoming mature

MEDUSA noun : a mortal Gorgon who had snakes for hair (note : to gaze upon her would turn one to stone)

METAMORPHOSIS noun [Gk metamorphosis, fr. metamorphoun (to transform), fr. meta (change) + morphe (form)] : change of physical form, structure, or substance

MIRACLE PLAY noun : medieval religious play based on the life of a saint or martyr (compare MYSTERY PLAY)

MONUMENT noun [L monumentum (memorial), fr. monere (to remind)] 1a : a lasting evidence, reminder, or example of someone or something notable or great   b : something erected (as a statue or building) in remembrance of a person or event

MOTHER TONGUE noun 1 : one's native language (one's native tongue)   2a : a language from which another language derives   b : a language from which other languages derive

MULIEBRITY noun [L muliebris (of a woman)] : FEMININITY

MUSICALE noun [soiree musicale (musical evening)] : social entertainment with the principle feature being music

MYSTAGOGY noun [mystes (initiate), akin to myein (to be closed) + agein (to lead)] : the practice of initiating another into a mystery cult — i.e., the vocation of the MYSTAGOGUE

MYSTERY PLAY noun : medieval religious play based on an event in scripture (e.g., The Passion of Christ; compare MIRACLE PLAY)

NECROPHILIA noun [nekros (dead body) +philia (friendship), fr. philos (dear)] : obsession with and usually erotic interest in corpses

NECROPOLIS noun [nekros (dead body) + polis (city)] : a large cemetery (especially of an ancient city)

NEOLOGISM noun [neos (new) + logos (speech, word)] 1 : a word, usage, or expression that arouses disdain do to its newness and/or barbarousness   2 : a word coined by a lunatic (often deemed meaningless)

NEPHILIM noun : a race of giants whose superhuman stature is the result of divine-human wedlock (see Num 13.33; Deut 2.10-11 — i.e., "the sons of God" marrying "the daughters of man")

NE PLUS ULTRA : LATIN = (GO) NO MORE BEYOND (i.e., the highest point and/or the most profound state capable of being attained)

NIGREDO : LATIN = BLACKENING (term used in alchemical manuscripts)

NOCTAMBULISM noun [L noct (nox = night) + ambulist (from ambulare = to walk) : the act, practice or condition of "sleep walking"

NOMENCLATURE noun [nomen (name) + calare (to call)] 1 : NAME (designation)   2 : a system or set of terms or symbols (often specific to a particular discipline, art, or science)

NOOSE noun [nodus (knot)] : a loop of rope with a running knot that tightens the more it is pulled

NOURISHMENT noun : FOOD, NUTRIMENT

NUPTIAL ODE noun [L nuptialis, fr. nuptiae (pl., wedding), fr. nuptus, pp. of nubere (to marry); akin to Gk nymphe (bride, nymph) + Gk oide (song)] : a lyric poem in honor of a marriage (see EPITHALAMIU)

OLD NICK noun : SATAN

OSCULATION noun [L osculatus, pp. of osculari, fr. osculum (kiss), fr. dim. of os (mouth)] : the act of kissing

OSTEOLOGY noun [oste (bone)] 1 : a branch of anatomy concerned chiefly with bones   2 : the bony structure of an organism

PAROLE noun [parabola (speech)] : a linguistic act (compare LANGUE)

PEDAGOGY noun [paid (child, boy) + agogos (leader)] : the craft, profession, or science of educating (especially the young) — i.e., the vocation of the PEDAGOGUE

PEDERAST noun [paid (child, boy) + erastes (lover)] : a man who enjoys having anal sex with boys

PENITENCE noun [paenitentia (regret)] : sorrow for sins or faults

POLYMORPHOUS PERVERSITY noun : taking the totality of the body (as opposed to specifics — e.g., cock, cunt) as eligible for erotic activity — i.e., having the whole body as an erogenous zone

PORNOLEXICOLOGY noun [porno (harlot) + lexis (word, speech)] (ca. 1910) 1 general : a branch of linguistics concerned with the signification and application of erotic and especially obscene words 2 specific : a branch of linguistics concerned with the signification and application of erotic and especially obscene words as a means to decipher the lewdness of Occidentalism —- see PORNOLEXICOLOGIST noun

POTABLE noun [LL potabilis, fr. L potare (to drink); akin to L bibere (to drink)] : a liquid suitable for drinking — especially an alcoholic beverage

PREDATOR noun : one that lives by predation

PREY noun : one taken by a predator as food

PRINCE CHARMING noun : a suitor who fulfills the dreams of his beloved (note : his beloved is asleep)

PRIVILEGE noun [L privilegium (law for or against a private person), fr. privus (private) + leg (lex = law)] : a right or immunity granted as a peculiar benefit, advantage, or favor (usually granted by reason of one's rank or one's office held

PROFLIGACY noun [pro (forward, down) + fligare (akin to fligere to strike)] : the state or quality of being PROFLIGATE (i.e., the state or quality of being completely given up to dissipation and licentiousness)

PULCHRITUDE noun [pulcher (beautiful)] : physical comeliness

PUTRESCENCE noun : the state of being PUTRESCENT (see PUTREFACTION)

QUEEN REGNANT noun : a Queen reigning in her own right

QUEENSHIP noun 1 : the physical state of being a Queen (rank) 2 : the personal state of being Queen like (regality)

QUEEN'S ENGLISH noun : standard, pure, or correct English speech or usage AND/OR substandard, impure, or incorrect English speech or usage

QUIETUS noun [ME quietus est, fr. ML, he is quit (formula of discharge from obligation)] 1 : something that quiets   2 : DEATH

RASCALITIES noun : the characteristics or actions of rascals (KNAVERIES)

RECITAL noun 1a : ENUMERATION   b : NARRATION   2 : concert given by an individual musician

ROPE noun : see NOOSE

ROSERY noun : a place where roses are grown

SADE, DE [SADE, Donatien Alphonse Francois, Comte de (1740-1814) — usually known as the "Marquis de Sade"] : French soldier, writer, and pervert (see SADISM)

SANGRIA noun [sanguis (blood)] : a kind of punch (usually served iced) made by mixing red wine, fruit juice, and soda water

SAPIENCE noun [sapere (to taste, be wise)] : WISDOM (sageness)

SCHOOLMARM noun : a female schoolteacher so strict as to adhere to any and all school rules (no matter how arbitrary)

SHEOL noun : in early Hebrew thought, the underworld, the abode of the dead, that place to which the "shade" of a person went at death (see Gen 37: 36; Sam 2: 6-7; 28: 13; 2 Sam 12: 23; Job 26: 5-6; Pss 6: 5; 16: 10; 88: 5-6; 139: 8; Ezek 31: 10-18; 32: 17-32; and Am 9: 2)

SHULAMITE : The Lover of King Solomon in The Song of Songs

SOIREE noun [soiree (evening period, evening party)] : a party held in the evening

SOMNAMBULISM noun : abnormal condition of sleep in which motor acts are performed (e.g., "sleep walking")

SOPOR : LATIN = DEEP SLEEP

SPECULUM : LATIN = MIRROR (e.g., instrument inserted into body passage for purpose of inspection, ancient bronze or silver mirror, medieval compendium of all knowledge)

SPHINX noun [akin to sphinkter (sphincter)] : a monster having wings, the body of a loin, and a woman's head (note : the SPHINX killed anyone unable to answer her riddle)

STRANGE WOMAN noun [title used for whore in Prov (King James Version)] : PROSTITUTE

SUCKLING noun : a young unweaned animal

SUPPER noun : the evening meal

SUPPLANTATION noun : supersedure of another (especially by force)

TETRAGRAMMATION noun [tetragrammatos (having four letters) fr. tetra (four) + gramma (letter)] : the four Hebrew letters usually transliterated YHWH that form a biblical proper name of God (compare YAHWEH)

THANATOS : GREEK = DEATH (compare EROS)

THEATRICS noun : staged or contrived effects

THEOPHILIA noun [theo (god) + philia (friendship), fr. philos (dear)] (ca. 1910) 1 : unusual admiration and affection for God (e.g., excessive worship of God; or — more important — the persistent feeling of being in the presence of a loving God)   2a general : obsession with and usually (unconscious) erotic interest in God   b specific : sexual perversion in which God is the preferred sexual object — see THEOPHILIAC noun, see THEOPHILE noun

TITANESS noun : a female titan

TITLE noun : an appellation of dignity, distinction, or preeminence attached to a person by virtue of rank, office, or privilege (APPELLATION, DESIGNATION)

TOUGH LOVE noun (see BULLY)

TRANSCRIBE verb transitive [trans (across, beyond, through) + scribere (to write)] 1a : WRITE DOWN   b : COPY   c : RECORD   d : PARAPHRASE   e : SUMMARIZE   2 : TRANSLATE

TRAVAIL noun [tripaliare (to torture)] 1a : TOIL   b : TASK, EFFORT   c : AGONY, TORMENT   2 : LABOR, PARTURITION

TRICHOLOGY noun [thrix (hair) + logia (doctrine : theory : science)] : the study and practice of caring for and dressing hair

TRYST noun [triste (watch post)] 1 : an agreement between lovers to meet   2 : an appointed place for lovers to meet

UEBERMENSCH : GERMAN = SUPERMAN (overman)

URSPRACHE : GERMAN = PRIMEVAL or ORIGINAL LANGUAGE

VERACITY noun 1 : TRUTHFULNESS   2 : ACCURACY

VERIDICALITY noun 1 : VERACIOUSNESS   2 : GENUINENESS

VIDE INFRA : LATIN = SEE BELOW

VIDE SUPRA : LATIN = SEE ABOVE

VIVISEPULTURE noun [vivus (alive) + sepelire (to bury)] 1 : the act or process of burying someone alive   2 : the act or process of being buried alive

WHORE noun [ME hore, fr. OE hore; akin to ON horr (adulterer) — more at CHARITY] : PROSTITUTE

WHOREDOM noun [ME hordom (sexual immorality, idolatrous practices), fr. ON hordomr (adultery), fr. horr (adulterer) + dom (judgment)] : PROSTITUTION

[text + texture + context = cunt]

BENJAMIN L. PEREZ (aka., Dr. Vostu) is a psycho-sexual deviant from California. He began writing *The Evil Queen* in San Fransico and finished writing it in Los Angeles. He is the product of dyslexia, insomnia, BDSM, and a battery of turbulent relationships with femmes fatales (beautiful women who have a penchant for dyeing their hair red and burning his property). His literary influences include Francois Rabelais, Pierre Guyotat, and Georges Bataille. Moreover, his favorite drink is the Bloody Mary, he earned his BA in Religious Studies from UC Berkeley (summa cum laude), and he is a Gemini. Feel free to email him at vostu@yahoo.com

www.ingramcontent.com/pod-product-compliance
Lightning Source LLC
Chambersburg PA
CBHW050509260626
47157CB00004B/1251